I0452056

STAIRWAY TO HELL

PIERCE MOSTYN PARANORMAL INVESTIGATIONS
BOOK 2

C W HAWES

CWH BOOKS

Copyright © 2018 by CW Hawes

All rights reserved.

No part of this book may be reproduced in any form or by any electronic or mechanical means, including information storage and retrieval systems, without written permission from the author, except for the use of brief quotations in a book review.

All characters in this book are fictitious, and any resemblance to actual persons, living or dead, is coincidental.

❀ Formatted with Vellum

In memory of my friend and mentor, John J "Jack" Koblas, who believed in me when I didn't believe in myself.

JOIN THE TEAM!

Become one of my VIP Horror Readers and you'll get the latest news from my world; plus exclusive content, free stories, and other good stuff.

Begin the adventure today and you'll get a copy of *The Feeder* (not available in stores) as my thank you.

Click, tap, or scan the QR code to become a VIP Reader today!

1

PIERCE MOSTYN WAS DREAMING. Not a pleasant dream by any means. One of those nightmares that are so very vivid and yet, upon awakening, cannot be recalled other than in the feeling of dread they leave behind upon the conscious soul.

In the distance he heard music and his name being called. An insistent nudging joined the music and the words now being spoken to him. Suddenly the dream-state vanished, and Mostyn remembered where he was.

"Damn it, Mostyn. Answer your phone before the neighbors complain."

He sat, picked up the smartphone, and said, "Mostyn." The clock on the nightstand informed him the time was 3:08 in the morning. In his ear he heard, "Bardon, here."

"Good morning, sir."

"Good morning, Pierce, my boy. And a very good morning it is indeed. Come in ASAP. Doctor Kemper with you?"

Mostyn cleared his throat. "Yes, sir."

"She's to come in as well. See you shortly."

The silence indicated the call was over, and Mostyn set his phone down.

"What is it?"

Mostyn looked over at Doctor Dotty Kemper. "How the hell does Bardon know about us? I mean, I thought we were being sufficiently circumspect that even God was in the dark."

"Pierce, dear, I guess that shows Bardon's voodoo is greater than God's omniscience."

"Huh. I guess so. Well, he wants us in the office pronto. You want to shower first?"

"We'll save time if we shower together."

"I doubt that. But I'm willing to give it a try."

————

The office of Doctor Rafe Bardon smelled of sweet Virginia pipe tobacco. Mostly because Bardon was rarely seen without a pipe in his mouth or in his hand. The decor of his office was nineteenth century British men's club. The Director of the Office of Unidentified Phenomena, or OUP, an agency so secret fewer than fifty persons in all of the vast federal bureaucracy even knew of its existence, sat at his large and heavy black walnut desk, puffing gently on a dark brown pot-shaped briar pipe. Across from him sat Pierce Mostyn and Dotty Kemper in an identical pair of Westminster tufted leather chesterfield chairs in dark chocolate. Bardon removed the pipe from his mouth.

"Either of you ever hear of Binger, Oklahoma?"

Mostyn and Kemper both shook their heads.

"Up through the nineteen twenties there were persistent reports of unnatural occurrences on a mound located not far from the town. A headless female specter at night and a male specter in the day. Because of persistent rumors of treasure, numerous men visited the mound. A few came back unscathed, a few more came back deranged, and more than a few never came back at all.

"The last visitor was in nineteen twenty-eight, an ethnologist by the name of Howard Langley. He claimed to have found a cylinder made of a strange and unknown metal, which contained a manuscript written by one Pánfilo de Zamacona y Nuñez, supposedly a conquistador with Coronado.

"Zamacona, according to the manuscript, had discovered a vast subterranean world inhabited by a highly advanced race of decadent and xenophobic beings. Langley, in his last visit to the Binger mound, claims to have actually gone into the mound, which proved to be an ancient passageway to the subterranean world of K'n-yan. However, something frightened him to such a degree that he dropped the cylinder containing the manuscript and thus it is lost."

"Sounds like a load of crap to me," Kemper said. "I mean, who in his right mind would take such a valuable manuscript with him back to where he found it? Why not keep it in a safe place?"

Bardon puffed on his pipe. "Perhaps the story is 'crap', as you say, Doctor Kemper. And the loss of the manuscript certainly places the story under much suspicion. Neverthe-less, Langley insisted on the truth of his account. He wrote it down, including a summary of Zamacona's adventure in K'n-yan. The account was found among his papers after his death. It was thought to be a story and was published in a magazine: *Weird Tales,* if memory services me correct, some-time in the nineteen forties. A while ago, this office acquired Langley's original manuscript. Of particular interest is the fact that the K'n-yanians, according to his tale, worshipped Cthulhu, Yig, Shub-Niggurath, and for a time the sublimely hideous Tsathaggua."

At the names, Kemper visibly blanched, and a shiver went through her.

"Are you all right, Doctor Kemper?" Bardon asked.

She swallowed and nodded. Mostyn, though, couldn't help but notice the tremors in her hands.

"Agate Bay was life altering," the Director said, his voice soft. "A shoggoth will do that to one."

Kemper nodded again, and uttered a barely audible, "Yes".

In a fatherly tone, Bardon said, "If you don't feel ready, you can sit this one out."

"No, I'll be fine, Doctor Bardon," she replied.

Mostyn asked, "Is the mound still there, sir?"

"No. After the Innsmouth episode, the Bureau of Inves-tigation, now known as the FBI, somehow got wind of Langley's story. That was in the early nineteen thirties. How they became aware of his account of the mound is unknown, but even back then Mr. Hoover was compiling the beginnings of the infamous X Files. So I suppose they had their ways, just as I have mine." Bardon paused and a smile touched his lips, then he continued.

"Anyway, the Bureau learned of Langley's tale. The US Army Corps of Engineers then moved in and completely leveled the mound. Nothing was noted in the official record if there was an entrance to a subterranean world or not. The mound was bombed, dynamited, and bulldozed into oblivion. Quite obviously, I think, especially after Innsmouth, the Federal government wasn't going to take any chances."

"Has something come up in Binger that you want us to investigate?" Mostyn asked.

"No. There's nothing there anymore. However, fifty miles to the northwest of Binger, near Oakwood, Oklahoma, is a Federal Department of Energy research facility on the west bank of the Canadian River, which is managed by Bessemer Corporation. The facility is in the middle of nowhere. Just farmland all around it."

"So what's the big deal?" Kemper asked.

"Work crews were breaking ground for an expansion of the facility, and uncovered an ancient staircase. Photographs of the bas-reliefs carved into the stone show images of debauchery, mutilation, and representations of Cthulhu, Shub-Niggurath, and Tsathoggua. In addition, since the uncovering, four workers have disappeared and have not been found. A fifth was missing for four days. He was discovered wandering the farm fields, his mind totally gone."

"What do you mean 'totally gone'?" Kemper asked.

"Just what I said. It's as though his personality was

wiped clean. He is under observation in a secret Federal facility. Our mission is to find out what is going on, determine if there is a threat to US security, and if there is, to neutralize it in order for the Department of Energy to continue work on expanding the research facility."

"Same old stuff," Mostyn quipped.

"Indeed, my boy, indeed." Bardon pushed a folder across his desk, and Mostyn retrieved it. "That is an abstract of the file on the Binger situation. The full file is on the computer. You have a flight at nine to Oklahoma City, where you will meet the other members of your team, and from Oklahoma City you will proceed by helicopter to the facility. You and your team members will have papers and cards identifying you as agents of the Department of Energy's Intelligence and Counter-Intelligence Division. That should give you free rein to do what needs to be done. Temporary housing is being moved onto the facility property as we speak. Any questions?"

"No, sir," Mostyn said, and Dotty Kemper shook her head.

"Very good. This situation if it is anything like that in Binger all those years ago could prove to be dangerous. There will be four Army military police and four Army Rangers available for your use should you require their services, as well as our special weaponry."

"Thank you, sir," Mostyn said.

"If nothing else, I wish you the best of luck." Bardon stood, and extended his hand. Mostyn and Kemper stood, shook hands with their boss, and left his office.

On the way to Mostyn's car, Kemper asked, "Do you think we'll run into...?"

"A shoggoth?" Mostyn completed her sentence for her.

She nodded.

He paged through the abstract before answering and when he'd reached the last page, he said, "No. No shoggoths. However, given what's in here—" He tapped the folder. "You might prefer one."

2

THE HELICOPTER TOOK OFF, and seven people watched it disappear over the eastern tree line. A uniformed military police officer approached the group.

"I'm Sergeant First Class Jerome Chestnut. I'm the commanding officer of the police unit here. Which one of you is Special Agent in Charge Mostyn?"

Mostyn raised his hand.

Chestnut advanced to him and extended his hand. Mostyn took it and nearly got his fingers crushed in the handshake.

"A pleasure to meet you, sir," Chestnut said.

"Likewise," Mostyn replied, left hand rubbing the fingers of his right.

"Let me show you all to your quarters."

The sergeant took the OUP team, masquerading as Department of Energy Intelligence and Counter-Intelligence agents, around to the back of the large building where two mobile homes were located. The prefab buildings were nestled in among the trees growing along the bank of the Canadian River. For having just been moved onto the property, they looked as though they'd been there for years.

Chestnut pointed to one of the buildings. Lettered in black paint by the door was "GAB 1". "For the ladies in your party, sir," he explained. "You men are in GAB Two."

"What does the designation mean?" Kemper asked.

"Guest Accommodations Building One, ma'am. The other being building number two."

Kemper nodded.

"There's a phone and a directory in each building," Sergeant Chestnut explained. "Doctor Obermaier will have dinner with you all in the cafeteria at six. I will be back before then to guide you to the cafeteria. Any questions?"

There were none, and Chestnut said he'd see them later and left.

Kemper turned to Mostyn and whispered, "Are we going to have to start addressing you as 'sir'?"

"Very funny, Dot," he whispered back. In a normal voice, he said, "Get settled. Beames, Slezak, and you, Kemper, come over to the guy's place in twenty for a pre-dinner meeting."

"Yes, sir, Captain, sir!" Kemper said, and saluted.

A chorus of "yes, sirs" and salutes followed. Mostyn shook his head, picked up his bag, and entered GAB 2, the men on his team followed, just barely suppressing their laughter.

The living room contained a television, sofa, loveseat, a couple of tub chairs, a small coffee table, and a couple of tiny end tables. To the immediate right of the entrance was the door to a bedroom, to the left was a kitchen and dining room. A backdoor exited from the dining room, and in front of it were a table and six chairs. Beyond the dining room was a bathroom and laundry facilities, and finally the other bedroom. In each bedroom were two single beds.

Mostyn turned to the other men, who'd been following him through the pre-fab house. "Baker and I will take this room. Zink, Jones, you get the other bedroom. Hopefully, the cafeteria is full service so we won't have to cook."

Special Agent Jones walked back to the kitchen. "Can any of you cook?"

Mostyn shook his head. Initial contact with the early thirty-something model for a Greek god had not impressed him. On meeting, Jones had announced, "I'm Special Agent Diesel Chance Jones." He then used two fingers to pull his sunglasses down his nose, and looking right at Kemper, had said, "But you can call me 'DC'." The last thing Mostyn needed on the team was a playboy.

Doctor Zink answered Jones. "I can cook. In fact, better than any woman. It's why I never married."

Jones looked over at the aging, somewhat out of shape archeologist. "Sure it is, you virile hunk of beefcake."

"What the hell would you know—," Zink began, before Baker cut him off.

"I can open cans and throw frozen stuff into the microwave. They do have a microwave, don't they?"

Jones asked, "What do they look like?"

"Jesus," Mostyn muttered. In his normal voice, he said, "Zink and I will cook, if we have to. I don't want chef's surprise, especially from you two." His eyes focusing on Jones and Baker.

"Geez, Mostyn," Baker protested. "What's wrong with canned baked beans?"

"Nothing, Willie Lee. Nothing. Better than ptomaine."

Mostyn retrieved his bag from where he'd left it in the living room when entering, and took it to his bedroom, Baker following suit. When they returned to the living room, Jones was stretched out on the sofa, his bag lying where he'd dropped it. Zink was missing. However noise was coming from the bedroom, which indicated he was most likely there. And in a few moments, he emerged to join the others.

There was a knock on the door.

"Jones, put your bag in your room," Mostyn ordered.

The tall, broad-shouldered agent grabbed his travel bag, tossed it into his room, and opened the door in answer to the knock. "Come on in, ladies!" he sang out.

Doctors Esther Beames, Candy Slezak, and Dotty Kemper joined the others in the living room.

"Have a seat everyone," Mostyn said. He looked over his team. Kemper and Baker he knew from long association due to previous assignments. Kemper was a renowned forensic anthropologist and Baker, an award-winning photographer. The others were all new to him. He mentally recalled their dossiers as he took them in.

Esther Beames, an ethnologist specializing in Native cultures, was a short woman with thick glasses and long black hair that she wore in a ponytail. She was three-quarters Native American, forty-eight, and single.

Candy Slezak, with a doctorate in linguistics, was very tall and slender. Her light brown hair was liberally high-lighted in hot pink. At twenty-nine, she had a face that was not at all difficult to look at.

Doctor Butcher Thomas Zink, at six feet even, could look Slezak in the eyes. He had a stocky build and, at fifty-two, was beginning to grow a potbelly. He was the other person on the team who wore glasses. He taught archeology, but was more often out in the field somewhere.

Special Agent "DC" Jones was everything Mostyn didn't care for in an agent. At six-three, with broad shoulders and narrow hips, he was an imposing sight. Add to that his blonde hair and blue eyes, and he could have been a Greek god, or a model for the cover of a romance novel. But it wasn't his physique Mostyn disliked; it was Jones's cock-sure attitude, and that the agent saw himself as Casanova's successor.

Regardless of his thoughts concerning any team member, they had a mission to undertake. Which meant they all had to rely on and support each other in order for it to succeed.

"None of you are new to OUP operations," Mostyn began. "I trust you've familiarized yourself with our mission and each other's dossier. Tomorrow we begin our exploration of the tunnel system the construction workers uncovered. Our mission is Code Red. And while I don't insist on formality, I do insist on obedience. Our lives may depend on it."

Beames raised her hand, and Mostyn indicated she

should speak. "By obedience, do you mean we can't question your decisions?"

"Unless I say otherwise, all decisions are 'me' decisions. I'm the one who decides."

"Why?" Zink asked.

"Because I'm in charge, and I'm the one Bardon will hold responsible if this blows up."

Zink smiled. "Okay, Boss."

Mostyn continued. "Depending on the situation, we may have a 'we' decision — one we all make together. Rarely, a 'you' decision, where I let you decide. First and foremost, on this mission, due to the potential for danger, I decide. Any questions?"

"What if we disagree?" Slezak asked.

"Keep it to yourself until we are in a safe environment, and then discuss it with me if you wish. Any other questions?"

Beames asked if there had been any other encounters with the K'n-yanians.

"No. At least not that we're aware of, aside from the Binger episode in the twenties," Mostyn replied. "Any other questions?" There were none, and he continued, "You all know your jobs. Hopefully, everything will turn out to be routine and I won't need to be the boss man. We'll find out tomorrow."

There was a knock at the door. Zink got up and answered it, letting in Sergeant Chestnut.

"If you all will follow me, Doctor Obermaier is looking forward to meeting you."

Mostyn stood, his team followed suit, and Chestnut led

the way across the lawn to the back of the building, where large windows of one-way glass looked out onto a patio. Chairs and tables were on the patio and in between the large windows were double doors. Chestnut held one of the doors open and Mostyn and his team filed inside.

Mostyn turned and looked out the windows, which afforded a view of the patio, lawn, and the tree line along the river. The room they were in was spacious. The tables, chairs, and lunch counter revealed it to be the company cafeteria.

Two men approached the team. Both were dressed in midnight blue suits. The younger of the two carried an iPad. The older man, who carried extra weight around his middle, had a distinctive Prussian air about him. When they reached the team, the older man introduced himself and his companion.

"I'm Fritz Obermaier and this is my assistant, Early Webster." Obermaier looked at Mostyn and said, "Special Agent in Charge Pierce Mostyn, I presume?"

"I am," Mostyn replied.

Obermaier extended his hand. "Pleased to meet you, sir." Mostyn took it, and they shook hands. He then introduced the other members of his team.

When all the handshaking was done, Obermaier waved his hand towards the tables. "Come, sit. We'll be served supper momentarily."

Zink inquired, "I take it you have a cafeteria because there's no decent place to eat around here?"

"Not within eighty miles." Obermaier replied.

Everyone took a seat. Obermaier was on Mostyn's left,

Dotty on Mostyn's right. Webster sat on the other side of his boss. Mostyn noticed a chalkboard by the counter with the day's entrées. He was famished and thought the baked chicken, cream of broccoli soup, and baked potato sounded good. When the server appeared and took their orders, he noticed Kemper ordered the poached cod and salad.

He whispered to her, "Fish? I thought Agate Bay would have cured you of seafood."

She cast a sideways glance at him and whispered back, "You can be a real prick sometimes."

Mostyn choked back a laugh as Kemper got the server's attention and changed her order to chicken.

From the server, Obermaier turned his attention to Mostyn. "Now, sir, what can you tell me about the mysterious stairway and our equally mysterious disappearances?"

"I'm afraid nothing at this point in time, Doctor Obermaier," Mostyn responded.

"Top secret?"

"Possibly. Mostly, though, because I don't know what we're actually dealing with here."

"I see. Well, you'll have your chance tomorrow."

"Yes, sir."

"May I ask what it is you do here, Doctor Obermaier?" Kemper asked.

"You may ask, Doctor Kemper; unfortunately, I can't tell you."

Dotty shook her head. "Damn bureaucracies."

Obermaier let out a laugh. "As you say, Doctor Kemper, as you say."

The food came, and the conversation moved on to more mundane topics. When the meal was over Obermaier excused himself, and he and Webster left.

"What do you make of Obermaier, Mostyn?"

He shrugged. "I don't know, Dotty. Seems like a nice enough guy. He's concerned about whatever's been uncovered. Probably wondering if it will be a problem for his work."

"Do you think this really is Department of Energy property and a DOE project?"

Mostyn chuckled. "Could be. Then again, the DOE might have leased this facility to anyone. Might be how the DOE makes up for budget shortfalls. Does it matter?"

"I guess not. A touch of irony that a top secret research facility was built on top of a top secret underworld civilization."

"It is kind of ironic at that."

3
———

SHORTLY AFTER SUNRISE, Mostyn and his team were peering into the excavation site. At the bottom, on one end, was the uncovered stairway.

"From here, the workmanship of the stone looks to be pretty advanced," Zink said, slipping a small pair of binoculars into a pocket.

Baker took several photographs of the stairway, the large pit, and the surrounding area. The staircase was about twenty-five feet below the surface of the ground.

"Let's go down and take a closer look," Mostyn said.

On one end of the excavation, was a ramp leading down into the large hole in the ground. The team walked down the ramp. Four Rangers and two military police remained above. There were no construction workers. They'd been sent home pending the outcome of the investigation conducted by Mostyn and his team.

"What was that?" Doctor Slezak said, her voice betraying a trace of fear.

"What was what?" Kemper called out.

"I felt something push against me," Slezak replied.

"That was Jones trying to get into your panties," Kemper shot back.

"I felt it, too," Doctor Beames said. "Perhaps there are spirits here."

"Ghosts?" Kemper said, her tone of voice taunting.

Beames stopped. "Don't you feel it?"

The others stopped and looked at her.

Beames continued, "The evil, the malevolence."

"Yes," Slezak said softly.

A wind sprang up, swirling dust and dirt around the group.

"Something's pushing me," Slezak cried out.

DC Jones rushed to her side, and the wind ceased as abruptly as it started.

"This isn't normal," Beames said, "There are evil spirits here."

Kemper guffawed. "Evil spirits. You can't be serious."

Beames was angry. "I am serious, Doctor Kemper. There is something very bad here."

"All right, ladies, now is not the time to argue," Mostyn said. "We have a mission to accomplish."

Mostyn started walking towards the opening where the stairway was located. Almost immediately a wind sprang up.

"Good God," Zink blurted. "It's as if something's trying to deliberately stop us from going to the stairs."

Kemper muttered, "Superstitious twits", charged ahead, pushed past Mostyn, and suddenly fell backwards.

He rushed to her side, and at the same time a shot rang out. Behind him he heard, "Did you see that?" And, "A ghost. I saw a ghost." Mostyn stood and looked up at the MP with his rifle trained on the stairway opening.

"What the hell is going on?" he demanded of the soldier.

"I saw a white shape, sir. It pushed, or seemed to push, Doctor Kemper."

Dirt and small stones were swirling about the opening. And then Mostyn himself felt as though something took hold of his wrist and was pulling him away, pulling him back the way he came. He shook his arm and took a step back. Dotty stood and went to his side, where both felt invisible hands, as it were, pushing against them. They looked at each other and then Mostyn gave the command to fall back.

Slezak and Beames ran up the ramp and out of the excavation site. Zink and Baker followed. Jones waited, pistol in his hand, until Mostyn and Kemper were halfway up the ramp and then he, too, followed, walking up the ramp backwards. Once everyone was at the top, the wind in the bottom of the excavation site ceased.

"Back to GAB Two," Mostyn ordered. "We need to talk."

———

Pierce Mostyn looked at his fellow team members sitting in the living room of the pre-fab house. Beames and Slezak truly looked as though they'd seen a ghost. The others looked puzzled trying to reconcile what they saw and felt with the normal and accepted laws of the universe. At last Mostyn spoke.

"Since I've been with the OUP, I've learned to reserve judgment on whatever I experience or think I experience. Doing so allows me to maintain a clear head. None of you are novices. I suggest you do the same."

"There's something evil out there, Pierce," Candy Slezak blurted out, while twisting her electric pink hair around a finger.

"Did you read the Binger report?" Mostyn asked.

Slezak nodded.

"Then why are you surprised?" he replied, and, taking them all in, continued. "Why are you surprised by what we experienced out there? You aren't green. This isn't your first mission. Get a grip, people. We are dealing with an unknown. We are the Office of Unidentified Phenomena. It's our job to identify the unidentified and figure out if it poses a threat to the good people of the United States of America.

"We're going back out there after lunch and this time I hope you have your individual and collective acts together. Do I make myself clear?"

Everyone either nodded their heads or made a verbal confirmation.

"Good. Now I'm going to talk to our trigger-happy guard and find out what he saw. Slezak and Beames, you're with me. Did anyone else see the apparition?"

No one indicated they had and Mostyn made for the door, signaling the two women to follow him. Out he went to the main building where he found Sergeant Chestnut's office and asked the sergeant to send him the MP who'd fired his rifle. He, Beames, and Slezak went down to the cafeteria to wait for the soldier.

Mostyn got coffee for the women and himself and the three sat at a table.

"Okay, ladies, what did this thing look like?"

"There was more than one," Slezak said.

Beames nodded, and added, "Diaphanous. White. Undulating, like the aurora borealis."

"They were barely visible," Slezak noted.

"How many?" Mostyn asked.

The women looked at each other before Beames answered, "Three." Candy Slezak nodded.

Mostyn sipped his coffee and appeared lost in thought. The women drank theirs in silence.

A man in uniform came up to them, black MP armband announcing he was military police. He stood at attention by the table. Mostyn looked up at him. He had private first class stripes on his shoulders and a name tag above his left breast pocket.

"Take a seat, Grundseth."

The man sat.

"All right, tell me what you saw that made you so trigger happy."

The private swallowed and said, "I can't rightly say, sir. It was some sort of white shape. But barely visible. I saw it push Doctor Kemper and she went down, the thing stepped back, and that's when I fired at it."

"Was it undulating?" Beames asked.

"Was it what, ma'am?"

"Undulating. You know, um, rippling."

Private Grundseth thought a moment and said he thought so.

Mostyn nodded. "Anything else, Grundseth?"

"No, sir."

"Very good. We'll be going back out there after lunch. This time try not to shoot unless it's something with more substance. Like a body."

"Yes, sir." Grundseth stood, saluted, and left.

"Thanks, ladies. We'll be back at it after lunch. Be prepared."

"Sure thing, Pierce," Slezak said.

Beames nodded.

Mostyn watched them go. He had a few preparations to make before lunch. Ghosts or no ghosts, they were going to explore that stairway.

4

AFTER LUNCH, Mostyn and his team were once again at the top of the ramp that led into the excavation pit. With the team were the four Rangers and two of the MPs.

Everyone was equipped with helmets and head lamps, goggles, body armor, and an assortment of firearms. The team's weapons included grenades, a flamethrower, a light machine gun, and a sonic disruptor as well. In their backpacks were tools and MREs. Everyone had a canteen of water.

Kemper's comment seemed to reflect everyone's mood. "With all this shit, we look like we're ready for a stroll in Kandahar Province."

"Or downtown Detroit," Baker added.

"All right, people," Mostyn began, "we're going down to the stairway. If we encounter any more nebulous creatures, Gibson, use the disruptor."

Private First Class Patty Gibson had the weapon in her hands. "How do we know this thing works?"

"Didn't Jones give you instructions?"

"He showed me how to turn it on."

Mostyn shook his head, looked at Jones, and then took in the excavation site. "Okay, see that rock over there?"

"Yes, sir."

"Power up the disruptor, make sure the selector is on narrow field, aim at the rock, and pull the trigger."

Gibson powered up the weapon. Rings along the barrel began to glow, making the thing look like something out of an old Buck Rogers movie. Gibson adjusted the selector, aimed, and pulled the trigger. There was a whine and then the rock vaporized into a cloud of dust."

"Does it work, Gibson?"

"Yes, sir. That was amazing."

"Shut it down so we can conserve the power unit."

Gibson powered down the disruptor.

"But what if it doesn't stop the ghosts, sir?" Grundseth asked.

"We'll deal with that situation if it happens," Mostyn replied. "Any other questions?"

There weren't any. Mostyn put on his goggles, and motioned for everyone to follow him. Into the large hole they walked. At the bottom of the ramp, the wind sprang up and began pushing against them.

"Anyone see anything or feel anything?" Mostyn called out.

"Just the wind," Slezak and several others replied.

Mostyn nodded and continued the walk towards the stairway. The wind picked up making the dirt and small stones feel like bullets pelting his body armor and helmet.

"They're here!" Beames called out. "I see them!"

At the same time Mostyn felt something push against him. "Fall back," he ordered.

They retreated about thirty feet and Mostyn confirmed with Beames and Slezak that the ghostly shapes were still present.

"They're there," Slezak replied.

"I see four of them," Beames added. "Directly in front of us."

"How far?" Mostyn asked.

"About thirty feet," Beames replied.

"Okay, Gibson, get to work."

PFC Gibson shouldered the sonic disrupter and powered up the weapon. There was a quiet hum and the rings around the barrel began to glow.

"I don't see anything, Mr. Mostyn."

"Beames, direct her aim," Mostyn ordered.

The Native American ethnologist guided the soldier's aim and Gibson squeezed the trigger. Once again they heard the high-pitched whine and then Beames said, "It's gone!"

"The others?" Mostyn asked.

"They fled," Beames replied. "Ran back to the stairway and down it."

Mostyn nodded, and smiled. "Okay, people, these aren't ghosts. They're human beings who've de-materialized. Remember the account from the mound at Binger?"

"Partly de-materialized disgraced freemen," Doctor Zink corrected.

"I don't think this bodes well for us," Doctor Beames said.

"It doesn't matter if it does or not," Mostyn admonished. "We have a mission and we are going to see it through. The security of the people of the United States depends on us."

"I didn't sign up for this," Doctor Slezak said. "I'm not a hero." Agent Jones moved next to her.

"Enough," Mostyn said, his voice quiet and stern. "And, yes, you did Slezak. You can resign when we get back from our mission. Right now I need your expertise."

She gave him a look that clearly indicated she wasn't at all happy over her expertise being needed.

Mostyn ignored it and continued, "Now, does anyone see anymore of these partly de-materialized guards?"

"No. They're gone." Doctor Beames's voice was full of resignation.

"They're just waiting for us down below," Slezak muttered.

"Follow me," Mostyn said, as he trekked off towards the stairway, dirt and pebbles swirling around him.

"What are you waiting for?" Kemper called out. "You want to live forever?" And she took off after Mostyn, not hearing Slezak's, "Yes".

Corporal Ellis said to the soldiers, "You heard the man. Forward, march!"

Zink sighed, and said, "We who are about to die, salute you!", and followed the others. The remaining team members, at Jones's urging, straggled towards the stairway after Zink.

Mostyn stopped at the top of the stairs and the wind suddenly ceased. He looked at the darkness into which the stairs disappeared. The inky stygian gloom exuded a nearly palpable evil. He turned on the powerful electric lamp attached to his helmet. The beam of light appeared to be absorbed by the dank smelling gloominess.

The others clustered around him. Baker snapped pictures, while Privates First Class Pettigrew and Grundseth added their helmet lights to Mostyn's in an attempt to pierce the gloom, but to little effect.

Doctor Zink descended several steps, took out a magnifying glass and a brush, and began examining the stonework and the worn bas-reliefs carved into the stone. After a few moments, he waved to Slezak and Beames. "Candy, Esther, what do you make of these designs?"

Slezak and Beames joined Zink in examining the worn and nearly faded patterns. While they were doing so, Mostyn addressed the others in the group.

"Corporal Ellis, I want Gibson and Tanner in the lead. We will need the disruptor and the flamethrower available should we meet anymore of these people and they turn hostile. Then you and Michelson, with the machine gun."

"Yes, sir," Ellis replied.

Mostyn continued, "Kemper, Baker, you two and I will be next. Beames, Zink, you two will follow. Jones, Slezak, you will follow Beames and Zink. Pettigrew and Grundseth, you two will be the rearguard. Any questions?"

"How far are we going?" Slezak asked.

"Until we get some answers," Mostyn replied. "Any other questions?"

Baker's flash went off, a click sounded, and the flash went off again.

Private First Class Patty Gibson asked, "If we see hostiles, do we shoot first?"

"We don't know, yet, for sure if these people are hostiles. The account from Binger indicated a fair amount of xenophobia. Consequently what we encountered earlier may have just been them protecting their turf, not an indication of actual hostility towards us. I don't want to be in a position where we shoot our way in, only to have to shoot our way out again. If we see any of these subterranean inhabitants, I want to give them the benefit of the doubt. Shoot only on my command. Understood?"

"Sure seemed hostile to me," Kemper said.

A look of exasperation flitted across Mostyn's face. "Does everyone understand you only shoot on my command? That includes you, Dotty."

There was a chorus of nodding heads and verbal affirmations, including a nod from Dotty Kemper.

"Are you people done examining that stonework?"

"Yes," Zink replied.

Baker's camera clicked, the flash brilliant in the gloom.

"All right then people, let's go!"

Down the stairs they went, which were wide enough to accommodate three people walking side by side. The combined illumination of their headlamps dispelled the gloom and they saw the stairway descend into the bowels of the earth.

"The masonry here is quite interesting," Zink commented. "The walls and stairs for the first thirty feet of our descent were made from basalt blocks. The builders then switched to limestone."

"Why?" Baker asked.

"I'm thinking because basalt was more difficult to find than limestone or sandstone," Zink explained. "I'm not a geologist, but ancient peoples tended to build with what they had on hand. This area of Oklahoma has plenty of limestone and sandstone that's fairly easy to obtain. So if the building project was ordinary, they would use what was available."

"Very true," Beames agreed. "For very special projects, they might import special stone."

"Agreed," Zink said.

"So why the basalt?" Kemper asked.

"More durable than limestone that hasn't been sealed against water," Zink explained.

"And they made the switch why?" Baker asked, snapping pictures of the grotesque figures in bas-relief decorating the walls. Unseemly monstrosities in various positions copulating with or eating humans. There were also images of human beings tortured by other humans and of humans in various coital positions.

Zink answered, "I suppose they felt less chance of water damage this far down."

"I suppose that makes sense," Baker replied, snapping more pictures.

"These people are sick," Kemper said. "Nothing but torture and fucking."

"What's wrong with fucking?" Slezak asked.

"Nothing," Kemper replied, "unless it's with one of

those godawful looking creatures." She stopped a moment to look at a human-sized frog copulating with a large-breasted woman. "Shit, that's sick," she muttered, and continued walking. After a moment, she added, "I suppose that's what was going on in Agate Bay."

"Yep," Mostyn affirmed.

Kemper shuddered.

Thirteen pairs of shoes and boots plodded on down the stairs. The pitch blackness finally fleeing before their lights. The deeper they went, the quieter everyone got until only the sound of shoes and boots on the stone was heard. In places, rivulets of water had eaten away the limestone blocks. Suddenly, the stairway ended and the limestone blocks gave way to carved natural rock. Mostyn ordered a halt.

"Let's take ten before continuing," he said.

Gibson and Tanner put their weapons down and sat on the rock floor. They took out their canteens and sipped water. Michelson set down the machine gun and leaned against the wall. Corporal Ellis made his way to the back of the group to talk with Pettigrew and Grundseth, who were leaning against the rock wall, drinking water.

Zink took the opportunity to examine the rock face. Beames sat, drinking from her canteen. Jones and Slezak were leaning against the wall talking very quietly to each other. Kemper and Baker sat, while Mostyn went to the back of the formation and took a long look back up the stairs. The entrance was a tiny pinpoint of light.

He turned around and asked, "Anyone have any idea how deep we are?"

Zink turned from his examination of the rock and looked back at Mostyn. "Based on rate of descent and distance travelled, I'd guess we're about seven, eight hundred feet below the surface."

Mostyn thanked him, and made his way back to the front of the formation, tagging Jones to join him. They walked about fifty feet ahead of the group.

Jones observed, "I'm surprised it's not stuffy down here."

"Yes, that is interesting." Mostyn examined the wall. "No sign of any sort of torch." He looked up at the rock which was about twelve feet above them. "No sign of soot on the ceiling, either."

"Odd. Don't you think?"

"I do, Jones, I do. They either don't use torches, or haven't been down this way often enough to leave marks."

"The stairs weren't worn from heavy use, either."

"No, they weren't." Mostyn looked down the tunnel. "Wider, here, too. We could stand six across easy." He took a final look around. "Okay, let's join the others. And Jones?"

"Yes, sir?"

"Just remember, this is a mission. Not *The Bachelor*. Got it?"

"Yes, sir."

"Good."

They walked back to the rest of the team, where Mostyn told everyone they were moving out and to stay alert. The team walked on down the tunnel which had a slight descending grade to it and thereby gradually took them deeper into the earth.

There were no bas-reliefs on the walls, although periodically a cartouche containing various figures and shapes had been carved into the rock. Slezak examined several and said that while they looked Egyptian, they weren't. When Mostyn asked her if she could read the inscriptions, she replied she'd never seen anything like them before.

Zink confirmed they appeared to be hieroglyphs from an unknown language, if they were indeed hieroglyphs; and Beames noted they weren't from any Native peoples she was familiar with, ancient or modern.

The team continued down the tunnel for about half a mile when it opened up into a very large chamber.

"Form a circle around me, everybody, and I want you facing outward," Mostyn called out. From the center of the circle, he was able to survey the lamplit chamber. He guessed the large room to be fifty feet in diameter and about forty feet high. Ninety degrees from the tunnel entrance, on both the left and right sides of the room, where large alcoves.

In the alcove on the right was a statue of Cthulhu on a pedestal. His hunched winged body and octopus head was carved out of some kind of iridescent green stone. The pedestal on which he sat was of some manner of black-colored rock.

The alcove on the left contained a statue of Shub-Niggurath, the Black Goat of the Woods with a Thousand Young. The figure carved in the black stone was of a goat's head with a female face, a woman's upper torso, with large pendulous breasts, and the arms of a woman and the legs of a goat. The pedestal on which the deity stood was the carven effigies of her myriad children.

Beames muttered, "That thing is positively grotesque."

Zink, who was standing to her left, said, "Welcome to insanity."

Kemper, who was standing across from Cthulhu, said, "That stone makes this thing look alive."

Baker, on her right, added, "Be thankful it isn't."

PFC Evan Tanner, to Baker's right, his voice containing a slight tremolo, said, "What is this place? What are these, these *things*?"

"That," Mostyn answered, "is the great Cthulhu. Now he sleeps. Pray to whatever you deem sacred he never wakes."

Jones was looking up. He called out, "Boss, does that look like soot on the ceiling?"

"Everyone look up," Mostyn ordered. With the combined effect of their lamps, he confirmed Jones's suspicion, as did Zink and Beames.

"Can we take a break?" Slezak asked.

"Take ten, people," Mostyn said. "Jones, with me."

With Jones following, Mostyn entered the tunnel directly opposite the one by which they'd entered the chamber. They walked about a hundred feet, Mostyn listening and studying the walls, floor, and ceiling.

"What do you think, Boss?"

"I don't know, Jones. Seems, to me, highly unusual that our diaphanous guards should simply disappear. Why wouldn't they want to stop our advance?"

"Maybe they want us here?"

"Yes, that's what I'm thinking."

"Maybe we ought to go back. Get reinforcements."

"That's one option. Although I only have two more MPs to draw from."

Jones started to speak and Mostyn held his hand up to silence him. After a moment, he asked, "You hear that?"

"Yeah, it sounds like the slapping of bare feet on stone."

"I think company's coming. C'mon!"

Mostyn ran back to the chamber, Jones following. He burst into the room. "Everyone, back into the tunnel! We've got company!"

In a mad scramble, soldiers and scientists rushed back the way they'd come. Mostyn called out, "Gibson, Tanner, Michelson, Ellis, you have the firepower. You'll be in the mouth of the tunnel. Jones and I will be behind you. Pettigrew and Grundseth, you're the rear guard. Listen up! If they attack and we can't hold them, the rest of you retreat. Get the hell out of here and back to the surface. Tell Obermaier to seal the stairway. Now get down, everyone!"

The team was in position in the tunnel and waited for whoever it was that was coming. They didn't have long to wait. Shambling into the chamber was a horde of beings, for human would be too generous a term for them.

Perhaps they'd once been human, but no human has two heads, or three legs, or five arms, or seven eyes. And no human has no head or the body of a four-legged animal. What was also apparent, was that they were ready for combat. In their hands were an array of spears, bows and arrows, swords, and maces.

Slezak screamed and panicked, thrashing about in an attempt to flee. It took both Zink and Baker to get her under control.

Mostyn, in a quiet voice said, "Tanner, get ready. Those, I'm guessing, are *y'm-bhi*. Think of them as being like zombies."

"Got it, sir," Tanner answered, and got his flamethrower ready.

To the group of beings in the chamber, Mostyn called out, "We mean no harm. I would like to speak to your leader."

There was no initial response, then after a few moments up came a bow with an arrow nocked to the string. Mostyn yelled, "Tanner, now!"

There was a click and then a stream of fire shot out of the barrel of the flamethrower, cutting through the zombie-like creatures, and hitting the opposite wall. PFC Tanner swung the barrel and, in the ten seconds that the igniter cartridge was burning, he'd reduced the living dead to a pile of smoking and charred flesh. He emptied the burnt out cartridge and put in a fresh one.

In a matter of moments, another hoard of the zombie-like creatures poured into the chamber and Tanner's flamethrower spewed out another wall of fire that reduced the ambulatory dead to a pile of smoldering flesh and bones.

"How many more of those things are there?" Corporal Ellis muttered.

Tanner looked back. "I don't know, Corporal, but I'm almost out of fuel."

"The spirits! The spirits!" Beames yelled.

"Fire, Gibson! Fire!" Mostyn ordered.

"Where? I don't see anything." Gibson's voice was shaking.

"Arc it!" Mostyn yelled.

She flipped the switch, the sonic disruptor powered up, and she pulled the trigger as fast as she could, swinging the big weapon in an arc across the chamber.

"Beames! Did she get them?" Mostyn asked.

"They're gone," Beames replied.

"Okay, people, let's get out of here," Mostyn commanded. "Back the way we came. And double-time it."

Thirteen people took off running back up the corridor. Suddenly Private First Class Pettigrew screamed, "They're here!" And both she and PFC Grundseth opened fire.

Mostyn pushed his way to what was now the front of the column. Seven bodies lay in the tunnel.

"They just appeared out of nowhere," Grundseth said.

Mostyn heard behind him the whine of the sonic disruptor and the crack of a pistol. In front of him a half-dozen figures materialized and in a second they were cut down by Pettigrew and Grundseth.

From the back of the column, came the whoosh of the flamethrower and then the whine of the disruptor.

More figures materialized in front of the column and they were quickly cut down by Pettigrew and Grundseth.

"Come on! Let's move it!" Mostyn yelled, and took off at a run up the tunnel with Pettigrew, Grundseth, and the rest of his team following.

Pistol and rifle fire came from behind and up ahead a

large group suddenly materialized. Pettigrew and Grundseth emptied their magazines and still more people materialized in front of Mostyn's team, blocking their retreat.

Ellis shouted, "The flamethrower's empty, there's no more charge for the disruptor, and we have ghosts up our ass. Dozens of them!"

Mostyn looked back and saw the partially de-materialized beings. They were clearly visible, but there was a filmy translucent quality about them. He turned around and saw the very large group of very physical men in front of him and then they were yelling and screaming as they charged.

Grundseth and Pettigrew got their rifles reloaded, but not before the attackers were on them and they were quickly overpowered. Mostyn threw a punch and caught one of the attackers before he could use his club. He put his head down and barreled into a man, who went down. Mostyn was on top of him and grabbed his club, using it to block a slash from a sword.

Suddenly there was only Mostyn, with half a dozen sword points mere inches from his chest.

5

MOSTYN FOUND HIMSELF, alone, in a simple room lying on a bed. He sat up, pushed the thin blanket aside, and swung his feet to the floor. He was naked.

Hopefully his captors would provide him with clothes. He wondered why they hadn't left him his own clothes. They were undoubtedly different than what the native inhabitants wore. They'd be just as good as prison garb.

He let his eyes take in his environment. The walls, ceiling, and floor were of white stone. On the floor were thick rugs. The colors were mostly shades of red and blue, black, and off-white. The room contained the bed on which he sat, a small table and two chairs made of some manner of woody fibers, a sofa, an upholstered chair, and a wardrobe.

There was a window covered with yellow curtains. He got up and walked to it. Pushing aside the curtains, he saw there was no glass in the window. The view was of a city. The buildings, he noticed, were also made of white stone and were not overly tall. Although a few looked to be more than ten stories high.

Everything was bathed in a bluish light and there was very little noise.

His room was four floors up from ground level and below him was a street. It wasn't exceptionally busy and the only traffic was pedestrian.

Turning around, he noticed the door in the wall opposite him. It was probably locked, but he wouldn't know unless he tried the handle. He walked over to it and it was indeed locked.

"A wardrobe usually means clothes," Mostyn said out loud, just to hear a voice. He walked to it and opened the doors. Hanging inside were three white robes. A pair of sandals were on the bottom of the unit.

He took a robe off a peg and slipped it on. The hem fell to his ankles. The fabric felt like linen. He slipped on the sandals, which were made of some kind of leather.

Next to the bed was a door. He crossed the room and turned the handle. The door opened to reveal a bathroom. There was a window, tub, commode, and sink.

"They have running water," he said to the stillness. "At least I won't have to rely on a chamber pot."

He closed the door and crossed to the upholstered chair and sat. The last thing he remembered was looking at six sword tips ready to make shish kebab out of him, when a tall man walked up and threw a powder into his face. He couldn't help but breathe some of it in and, when he did, he sneezed and that was that. The next thing he knew he was waking up in a strange room, obviously a prisoner.

The question uppermost in his mind was what happened to his team members. Were they alive? If so, were they being held prisoner in similar rooms? And Dotty. Where was Dotty?

His mind went back over the testimony of Howard Langley and his account of the supposed conquistador Pánfilo de Zamacona y Nuñez. If they were in the subterranean land of K'n-yan, and if Zamacona's tale, via Langley, was even remotely true, things did not bode well for Mostyn and the members of his team. The best they could hope for was to die a natural death being the permanent guests of the K'n-yanians. The worst was a hideous death in an amphitheater providing entertainment for their captors.

Mostyn sat in his brown study for some time until a shimmering in the air in front of the door aroused his attention. He watched three men materialize in front of him. They wore white robes. The one in the middle wore a gold circlet in the shape of leaves on a vine. He was unarmed. The other two men were armed with spears and swords. The man in the middle had an intelligent face. The two on either side of him looked like mannikins.

Mostyn stood. In his mind appeared the question, "Are you the one called 'Mostyn'?" He tried to form a picture of himself in his mind. The man across from him remained impassive. In succession, Mostyn nodded his head, said "Yes", and said "Sí".

At the word "Sí" the man's face showed recognition.

In Mostyn's mind came the question, "How do you know about us?"

To respond, Mostyn tried to picture the Binger mound, pictures of which he'd seen in the case file.

Apparently he was successful this time because the man with the gold circlet exhibited a cruel smile and said, "Zamacona".

"Sí, yes," Mostyn replied. In rapid succession, he pictured his team members. In reply came images of them in rooms nearly identical to his own.

Mostyn pictured himself visiting them and in response came a very clear "no". He walked over to the window and pointed outside. In his mind he pictured a nuclear explosion.

The face of the man with the circlet registered alarm, but only briefly.

To Mostyn's mind came a flood of images and information, the gist of which was Mostyn and his people were the aggressors and must now pay for their crime. How they were to do so had yet to be decided.

Mostyn tried to picture he was sorry and that they'd only attacked out of fear. If he and his companions were set free, no one would bother the K'n-yanians again.

The man replied that setting them free was not his decision. They would be questioned by the Council of Executives and the council would decide their fate. Until the council called for them they would remain prisoners.

Mostyn attempted to protest, but the three men disappeared, and he was once again alone.

6

MOSTYN WAS FRUSTRATED AND ANGRY, mostly at his own impotence to do anything. He stood at the window and looked out over the city, which according to the Binger file was named Tsath.

Four stories up there would be no jumping out the window to freedom. Unless one considered death freedom, and Mostyn did not.

The people down below on the street, bathed in the curious blue light, were oblivious of his existence and of the world that lay above the distant vaulted ceiling of stone.

Yet what if they knew? They had welcomed Zamacona and made him one of their own. Then when his desire for freedom became too much, they mutilated him to death, and since that wasn't enough, they reanimated his corpse so it could perform guard duty at the Binger gateway.

The air was warm, reminding Mostyn of San Diego or southern Italy. And according to the Binger file, rain did fall in the land of K'n-yan. He thought the immense cavern must be similar to the old zeppelin hangers which were so large clouds often formed and rain would fall. Probably plenty of water, but how did plants grow without sunlight?

Suddenly he smelled roasted meat and turning around, saw four plates of food and a goblet of blue-red fluid on the table.

"Damn useful their ability to dematerialize and rematerialize items," he said out loud, though no one was there to hear him. "They never have to open the door and I never get the chance to jump them."

He walked over to the table and looked at the food.

On one of the plates there was a thick slice of meat, covered in a gravy. Next to it was a mashed whitish vegetable. He tasted it and was reminded of cassava or taro.

On another plate was a cooked vegetable that was bluish-green in color and something that Mostyn guessed was a sautéed fungus. The vegetable was round like peas and the taste reminded him of lima beans. The fungus had a very mild nutty flavor.

On the third plate was a raw blue leafy vegetable that reminded him of radicchio. It was dressed with some kind of oil.

The final plate contained what looked and tasted like flatbread.

Mostyn sat and ate everything but the meat. It smelled delicious. However, he recalled in the Binger file that Zamacona supposedly recorded the K'n-yanians principally ate the flesh of a not quite human slave class and Mostyn decided he wasn't hungry enough to go cannibal and eat slaves.

He took a sip of the blue-red liquid. "Huh," he muttered. "Tastes like a pretty decent zinfandel or shiraz." He held the glass up to the light filtering in from the window. Definitely blue, shading to red. "Then, again, it just might be the blue light," he said out loud.

Mostyn pushed his chair back and with wine glass in hand got up and went over to the window. Tsath was a big place. From the window he was unable to see any of the countryside. He took a sip from the glass and then a second. The food was good. If they let him and his people live, they wouldn't starve. There was at least that.

He walked over to the upholstered chair and sat. The nagging question in his mind was if he'd see his people again. Would he see Dotty again? He drank wine. Dotty Kemper. Irascible and contrary though she could be, he was truly fond of her. While she was recovering from the shock and stress of seeing for the first time the living blasphemy of nature that is a shoggoth, he'd visited her. That's when he found out she was very fond of him as well. They spent Christmas together and had continued seeing each other. They weren't exactly living together and they weren't exactly not living together either.

The air in front of the door began shimmering. Mostyn stood and four men materialized in front of him. He chuckled. Star Trek had nothing on these people. Right now he'd give anything to be able to say, "Beam me up, Scotty," and get the hell out of K'n-yan.

One of the men shuffled over to the table and retrieved

the plates and tableware. He then dematerialized and was gone.

The man with the gold circlet was the same one as before. If the mannikin guards were the same, Mostyn couldn't tell. Mannikins all seem to look the same. He also took note of the distance between the wall and where they had materialized. Never know when such information might be useful.

The man watched Mostyn, his face registering no emotion. The mannikins simply looked straight ahead, eyes not focused on anything in particular.

Mostyn looked the leader in the eyes and sent happy, welcoming thoughts to him.

The man replied with what Mostyn took to be a standard formulaic greeting and proceeded to inform him the Council of Executives would see him now.

Mostyn finished off the wine, set the goblet down, and thought of his host leading the way.

A terse smile appeared on the man's face. He knocked on the door. It opened into the room, and the man walked out, indicating Mostyn should follow.

Outside the room, Mostyn saw he was in a wide hallway. From sconces on the wall, a blue-white light shone that brightly illuminated the corridor. In the lead was the man with the golden ivy circlet, followed by two guards, one of whom had opened the door, then Mostyn. The two guards who'd been in the room with the leader followed behind Mostyn.

They walked and walked. The corridor seemed without end. The walls, floor, and ceiling were of the same white stone which formed his room. The only decorations on the walls were the light fixtures. Periodically a door punctuated the sameness of the walls.

Pierce Mostyn looked at the doors as he walked passed. Were the rooms empty? Was a team member imprisoned within? The situation seemed so hopeless. Yet, unless he was dead, the situation was never hopeless. If these K'n-yanians were people, no matter how superior or inferior, they were fallible. He just had to find their weakness, or a single misstep and exploit it to his advantage.

The man with the golden circlet turned a corner and in a moment, when Mostyn did the same, he saw before them a grand staircase. Without hesitation the man descended the stairs, and the guards and Mostyn followed.

The staircase ended in an exceedingly large hall. There, Mostyn got his first close-up look at the general populace of K'n-yan. For in the hall were perhaps a couple dozen men and women. Some sitting, some walking, others in groups talking. Their facial features reminded him of Native Americans, yet there was also a difference that he couldn't put his finger on which immediately made one aware that these people weren't Native Americans. Their skin tone was uniformly pale, which made sense seeing that they lived without sunlight.

Upon becoming aware of Mostyn's presence, they stopped whatever they were doing and watched him go by. On his part, he observed them as well. There was a sameness of clothing, marked only by subtle differences, which perhaps indicated some manner of rank amongst them.

One woman in particular caught his attention. Her skin

was of the purest alabaster hue and her hair, which was the color of the darkest raven, fell to her waist. Their eyes met and Mostyn felt in his mind pity for him. He also felt an undeniable wave of intense lust wash over him and the thought that she hoped to be able to provide him with a sexual last supper, as it were.

Perhaps Zamacona was on the money in his understanding of these people. At least as Langley had passed on the Spaniard's thoughts. Their long lives, according to Zamacona, led them to having a deeply felt sense of ennui and an ever increasing desire to plumb the depths of depravity, hoping the new thrills would relieve their boredom.

Mostyn considered this. Their desire for new thrills and experiences might just prove to be his ticket for survival. If he could provide those thrills and experiences. And if he could survive, he'd find an opportunity to escape.

His warder made for two sets of large double doors and as he approached the set on the right, they were opened by two women who were as expressionless as his guards. Through the open doorway they went out of the building and onto a wide sidewalk next to the street.

The man with the circlet of gold turned right and Mostyn had no choice but to follow him, the guards ensuring he did not stray. They walked for a dozen blocks before turning into another building not unlike the one in which he'd been imprisoned. People on the street stopped and stared as he walked by and Mostyn chose to ignore them.

Inside the new building, they proceeded across the

stone tiles of the immense atrium to a set of doors, which gleamed golden in the blue-white light. The man knocked and they opened into a vast room, in the center of which was a long table at which sat nine men. Mostyn's party advanced until the man with the golden circlet stopped before a man seated in the center of the row of nine.

The seated men wore robes of blue and each wore a gold band on his head which was studded with blue stones. So this must be the Council of Executives, Mostyn thought. He looked around the vast hall. It was lit by the blue-white light coming from sconces on the walls and from large chandeliers suspended from the ceiling, perhaps thirty feet above them.

The man in white, Mostyn's warder, motioned for him to advance. Mostyn looked around him and then walked forward until he was standing next to the man he viewed as his jailer and across from the man in the center of the seated row of executives. Mostyn guessed him to be the chief executive.

The man, the chief executive, looked Mostyn in the eyes. "You are Mostyn. The leader of the invaders." It was as if the man had somehow gotten into Mostyn's head and whispered the words directly to his brain.

"No," Mostyn replied vocally. With his mind he tried to throw his thoughts so the chief executive could read them. "We're not invaders," was the message he tried to convey.

"Are you the man called 'Mostyn'?" The question appeared in his mind.

"Yes," Mostyn thought back.

"You refused to heed the warning and invaded our territory. How, therefore, are you not invaders and a danger to us?"

"Your people attacked us and we defended ourselves. My mission is to find out if you are a danger to the people of the United States of America."

"We know nothing of this 'United States of America'. Are we a danger to you?"

"I don't think so. Your weapons are inferior to ours."

"You have no idea of our power. We are, however, no threat to the world above. We simply want to be left alone. Ger-Hy'la-T'la," he motioned to the man next to Mostyn, "has told us you are aware of Zamacona, the last of your world to sojourn amongst us."

Mostyn nodded his head and verbally said, "Sí."

The eyes of the chief executive narrowed for a moment and then his face returned to impassivity. "To execute all of you would deprive us of much knowledge. This council has spoken with all of your companions. The decision has been made to execute your soldiers."

"No!" Mostyn said, the word was almost shouted. Taking a deep breath, he thought, "Take me instead. I'm their commander."

"Precisely," the lead executive conveyed to Mostyn's mind, and a slightly sinister smile appeared on his face. "There is no better way to torture a commander than to make him witness the deaths of those in his command. And when you do, know that you and you alone will save the others by urging their acceptance of their and your sentence. Namely, that you remain here as our guests until you die."

Mostyn's hands were balled into fists, which he held at his side. He said verbally through clenched teeth and then thought, "We meant no harm."

"But you did harm. Be thankful you who will survive have the privilege of living out your lives amongst the most advanced civilization in the world. And be warned — you will not have a second chance as did Zamacona should you try to escape."

Mostyn shoved Ger-Hy'la-T'la to the side and lunged forward, hands extended, ready to throttle the chief executive's neck. However, much to his surprise, the mannikin guards struck him down before he could get anywhere near the man's throat. Mostyn fell to the stone floor and the guards, grabbing hold of his arms, hauled him to his feet. He was furious. He looked at the man in blue, with the blue stone-studded circlet of gold, and sent thoughts of missiles, tremendous explosions, and devastated cities to his mind.

The man uttered a wicked and cruel laugh. In Mostyn's mind arose images of Cthulhu, Shub-Niggurath and her myriad young, and the ultimate hideousness of Tsathoggua. They were hovering over a barren wasteland ruled by eternal night. It took Mostyn a moment to realize the wasteland was the surface of the planet earth.

7

MOSTYN LAY ON HIS BED. Did the K'n-yanians actually have the ability to summon the Great Old Ones? Or was the executive bluffing? If they did, then the mythos, as currently understood, was in serious need of revision. If he was bluffing, and Mostyn guessed he might be because of the reaction of Ger-Hy'la-T'la when he'd sent him a picture of a nuclear device exploding, then they were vulnerable to First World technology — in spite of their advancements.

A slight breeze moved the curtain. Mostyn had no idea as to the time. The K'n-yanians had taken his watch. Thus far, he'd detected no change in the temperature. No change in the bluish light. Both were constants. He sat up and walked to the window.

He looked out over the city. He felt so helpless. He had no idea where his people were and no idea how they could escape. And if they didn't escape soon, six good people were going to die. Six men and women who were his responsibility. He balled his hands into fists and turned around. His eyes swept the room. It was so spare.

His eyes rested on the chairs at the table. He strode over to them, took hold of one of the chairs, lifted it high over his head, and hurled it onto the rug covered stone floor. It didn't break.

He picked it up and threw it against the wall. Picked it up again, swung it with all his might against the wall. The chair shattered. He picked up a leg and threw it across the room and out the window. He picked up the back of the chair and hurled it towards the window. It hit the sill and bounced back into the room. He went over to the broken piece of furniture and hurled it out the window; watching it fall to the street below, narrowly missing someone on the sidewalk.

His chest was heaving. "Get a grip, Pierce," he said out loud. "Destroying the furniture and killing a civilian isn't going to get you out of here. And you do want to get out of here."

He walked over to the sofa and threw himself on it. Could he have done anything differently? Probably not. The mission meant he had to make contact. Little did he know that the episode on the surface with the dematerialized beings was the contact he sought — and it wasn't friendly. If he had realized what had happened, he would have talked with Bardon and come up with a different plan. Too late for all of that now. He'd gotten his people into this mess and he needed to get them out. But how?

There was a soft knock at the door.

"Well, this is new," Mostyn murmured. He got up, went

to the door, called out "Entrar", and positioned himself so he'd be behind the door when it opened.

The air shimmered about three feet inside the room and then he saw the back of a woman wearing a pale blue robe. Her black hair reached her waist and because the robe was not loose and flowing, Mostyn guessed her hair hid a belt that cinched in the material.

Swiftly he moved up behind her, slipped his right arm between her arm and her body, brought his hand up behind her neck, and pushed her head forward. His left hand grabbed her left arm and pulled it behind her back. All that took no more than three seconds for Mostyn to accomplish.

She cried out verbally, "¡Ay!" Then her voice became seductive. "¿Vas a hacerme daño? Por favor, hazlo. ¡Una nueva experiencia!"

Mostyn couldn't believe his ears. He released his hold on her and turned her around. Speaking in Spanish, he asked, "You want me to hurt you?"

She replied in Spanish, "Oh, yes! We inflict pain on the slaves, but not each other. How wonderful to feel pain from one who were to bed me. A new experience!"

Mostyn's face registered surprise, and in Spanish he said, "Bed you? Who are you? And why would I bed you?"

She put on a pout. "You do not recognize me? We spoke in the entrance hall downstairs.

Suddenly Mostyn realized that in front of him was the woman who had made plain her desire for him. "I guess now I do, although I don't recall us 'speaking'."

She turned and walked away from him, then turned around and said, "I suppose not; however, I sensed a willingness on your part to enjoy me." She walked back to him and laid her right hand on his chest. "I like foreigners. Pánfilo was exciting. Different. I think you will be, as well."

Mostyn pushed her away. "Where I come from, um, men and women take some time to get to know each other."

"Oh? Get to know each other." She said the words as if the concept was foreign to her. "But you do enjoy each other, don't you? You like to feel orgasms, don't you?"

"Yes, we do."

"Oh, very good! Pánfilo did as well. Although he had this strange emotion. He called it 'guilt'. Do you feel this 'guilt'?"

"Sometimes."

"Will you feel guilt when I bed you?"

"Wait a minute. I don't even know your name."

"I'm called H'tha-dub. What are you called?"

"Most people call me 'Mostyn'."

"What do the others call you?"

"Pierce."

"How delightful!" She cocked her head to one side and slowly said his name, as though she were tasting wine. "Mostyn. Pierce." She undid the gold belt at her waist and let it fall to the rug covering the stone floor. She slipped her robe over her head and stood before Mostyn naked.

His eyes ran over her body. The alabaster skin. Her small, pert breasts. Her womanhood covered in black hair.

"Have we gotten to know each other?" She went to the bed and lay on it. She motioned for Mostyn to come to her. "Ven a mí Mostyn Pierce y fóllame."

He picked up her robe and belt, walked to the bed, and handed them to her. "No, we haven't gotten to know each other, and I'm not having sex with you."

Her face registered complete surprise. "You, you don't want me? You don't hunger for me?"

"You're very attractive, but, like I said, I need to get to know you first. So why don't you get dressed and we continue this conversation another time. Maybe tomorrow."

Her face was filled with puzzlement. "You don't like looking at my body? Is it ugly to you?"

"No. You have a fine body." He took a deep breath. "Maybe too fine."

"I don't understand." And then her face brightened. "Is this a game? To make me suffer from longing?"

Mostyn thought a moment. "Yeah. Perhaps it is."

"You foreigners. Your ways are so mysterious and exciting. Such new sensations!" She put the robe back on, handed Mostyn the belt, and backed into him. "Oh, Mostyn Pierce, you are a devil. And you *are* excited."

Mostyn put the belt around her waist and fastened it. She turned to face him.

"I shall play this game, Mostyn Pierce. I shall enjoy this pain of suffering, and then you will pleasure me and turn the pain into ecstasy!" She kissed him and dematerialized.

Mostyn stood looking at the empty air, then shook his head, and in English said, "Shit."

8
<hr />

THE INSISTENT KNOCKING at the door woke Mostyn from a sound sleep. A moment passed before he realized where he was. He swore under his breath and shouted in English, "Go away!" The knocking stopped. Satisfied that his tone of voice if not his words had conveyed his message, he turned over and attempted to go back to sleep. However, a voice disturbed his attempt.

"Debes despertar. Usted debe ser testigo de la ejecución."

"Like hell I do." There was no way this side of the lake of fire Mostyn was going to voluntarily witness the murder of his people.

Suddenly he was surrounded by four men who picked up his struggling body and hauled him out of bed to face Ger-Hy'la-T'la.

"On the other hand, maybe I will," he muttered.

The K'n-yanian informed Mostyn by way of telepathy

that he had no choice. If he didn't voluntarily witness the deaths of his people, he would join them.

Mostyn's looks and thoughts had all the intent to kill that Mostyn could muster. Nevertheless, the K'n-yanians did not expire, and the one holding a robe held it out to Mostyn, indicating he should take it. He grabbed the clothing from the man and stormed off to the bathroom.

In a few moments, having performed his morning toilet, Mostyn returned to face his jailer. Although he didn't look him in the eyes. Probably best if the K'n-yanian didn't see his thoughts right now.

Ger-Hy'la-T'la guided Mostyn and the guards out to the street where they climbed aboard a carriage drawn by four hideous creatures that were clearly not human and yet had a vaguely human countenance. Perhaps the semblance to humans was due to their facial structure, in spite of the horn protruding from the foreheads of the beasts, or that their four legs ended in paws that possessed a certain look that made Mostyn think of hands and feet.

In any event, a disquietude settled upon Mostyn after his viewing of what could be nothing more nor less than a foul degeneration of the human species into a ghastly abhuman beast of burden.

Ger-Hy'la-T'la informed Mostyn that the odd beasts were called *gyaa-yothn* and had been found running wild in the abandoned world of Yoth that lay below K'n-yan. "They are quite harmless," Ger-Hy'la-T'la said, via telepathy, "in spite of their somewhat ferocious looks and their carnivorous diet. They even have a rudimentary intelligence. Some of our learned ones are of the opinion the *gyaa-yothn* are actual descendants of the people of Yoth."

Mostyn thought back to his reading of the Binger file. He recalled Langley had written Zamacona was of the opinion that it was due to the rudimentary human intelligence of the *gyaa-yothn* that the K'n-yanians had been alerted to his presence in the first place and that it was one of the Spaniard's own beasts that had torpedoed his attempt to escape.

He watched the hideous monstrosities plodding along, pulling the carriage to whatever the destination. Beasts of burden that could be just as deadly as the most concealed and determined spy. He would have to remember that when his own time to escape presented itself.

Through the streets of Tsath the carriage travelled. Mostyn took note of the route, committing it to memory as best he could. Such information could possibly prove very useful when it came time to escape.

And Mostyn was very much intent on succeeding where the Spanish conquistador had failed. In fact, Mostyn had no choice. If the executive was telling the truth, getting caught attempting to escape was an immediate death sentence.

After a time, the carriage left the city proper and Mostyn saw the amphitheater. It was a circular structure, not unlike the famous Coliseum. An imposing edifice, quite easily capable of holding many tens of thousands of K'n-yanians.

The building was surrounded by a park. The plant life was strange and unfamiliar. Certainly not like any grass, trees, or shrubs in the world he knew. The foliage was a uniformly strange greenish blue, which prompted Mostyn to speculate the origin of the plants to be some specimen that had once lived in a prehistoric world on the surface. And had somehow morphed into what he now saw before him. The remaining chlorophyll a testimony to the one-time need for sunlight. A need now long gone.

The carriage pulled up a drive and stopped. The K'n-yanian, Mostyn, and the guards stepped down onto the pavement. Ger-Hy'la-T'la led the way into the amphitheater, up a broad staircase, to the second level, and then along a broad hallway to a door which opened into a room with seats. To Mostyn's surprise, his team members had preceded him. What was painfully obvious was the absence of his soldiers. Although the room was filled with K'n-yanian soldiers.

When Dotty Kemper saw him, her face lit up and she jumped up out of her chair and ran to him. Her arms went around him and she pulled him into a deeply passionate kiss.

There was a chorus of comments, a cheer or two, and a round of applause. Mostyn's face flushed, matching his strawberry blond hair. He joined the group, Willie Lee Baker making room so Mostyn and Kemper could sit together.

Ger-Hy'la-T'la addressed Mostyn and his people in Spanish. "You are aggressors and what you are about to witness is the punishment given out to those who harm the people of K'n-yan. Let this be a warning to you. Live here peacefully and you will have a good life. If you prove to be a threat, then today will show you your fate."

Doctor Beames asked in Spanish, "What will happen to us?"

The K'n-yanian replied, "You will be confined to your rooms. However, you will not be alone. Our scholars will meet with you to learn of your world and you will each be assigned to an affection group. You will only be able to go about the city or countryside when accompanied by one or more of your affection group."

"In other words," Mostyn replied, in Spanish, "we're prisoners. Will we be able to visit with each other?"

"No. You will not be allowed to visit with one another after today. We cannot take any chances."

"That's not right!" Doctor Beames said, her voice tinged with fury.

"Right?" the K'n-yanian shot back. "You had no right to come to our world. We warned you to stay away and you disregarded the warning."

"How will I be able to ensure the compliance of my people if we aren't together?" Mostyn asked.

"Once every other day, you will meet with one of your people to insure their compliance. If any choose to disobey you, they will die and you will lose a part of your body."

"Will someone please tell us what's going on?" Kemper said. "I, for one, don't know Spanish."

"Whatever it is they're saying, it can't be good," Slezak added.

Mostyn told the group what Ger-Hy'la-T'la had said. Slezak began crying, Jones's face registered no emotion, Zink muttered something about his work, Baker said,

"God. Poor Lisa", and Kemper, looking at Mostyn, softly uttered the words, "No. Please, no."

After a moment passed, Mostyn said, "You are my team. From today on, we are following Plan Epsilon. Understood?"

There was general assent.

The K'n-yanian spoke. "The entertainment begins. Watch. If you do not, you will join your fellows."

Mostyn looked out onto the floor of the amphitheater. The place looked an awfully lot like a surgical theater for teaching students who were studying to become doctors.

The first three brought into the theater were PFCs Josh Michelson, Evan Tanner, and Patty Gibson.

Tanner, who'd operated the flamethrower, was tied upside down to a pole and wrapped in black strips of cloth until only his head remained. His feet were set on fire and the blue flames slowly advanced down his body. He was a living torch and his screams echoed throughout the building until the flames reached his knees, when he apparently passed out.

The other two soldiers were each tied to a metal table. Gibson was screaming her head off and Michelson was trying to comfort her. The acoustics in the place were excellent. Mostyn could hear every word as if they were sitting next to him.

Speaking in the K'n-yanian language, one of the executioners held up a metal device and the crowd cheered. Another executioner held up a clamp and walked over to Michelson.

Michelson's voice was loud and clear and filled with panic. "Wait! No! What are you—"

His words were cut off as the torturer with the clamp grabbed Michelson's tongue and the other executioner-torturer cut it off. A third person held a tray into which the tongue was deposited.

Next they turned their attention to Gibson. Her screams turned to whimpered pleading. A conversation ensued between the spectators and the two torturers. After a few moments, they proceeded to sew Gibson's mouth shut.

Slezak threw up and tried to escape. Two of the guards grabbed her arms and returned her to her chair. She struggled until one of them put his sword point between her eyes.

"You hurt her," Mostyn said in Spanish to Ger-Hy'la-T'la, "and I will end your immortal life here and now."

He smiled and looked Mostyn in the eyes. In Mostyn's mind the words appeared, "You are brave. To be willing to die to save one of your people. Very well. You will only have to hear them and see the results. I think that will be sufficient."

Without any words being spoken, two of the guards drew thick black curtains across the large glassless window, blocking the view to the stage. They did nothing to block the sounds coming from the surgical arena, however.

The screams, cries, and curses of the men and women who had been under Mostyn's command rang throughout the amphitheater. Mostyn clenched his fists and gritted his teeth. Dotty, next to him, uttered a string of curses fit for a drunken sailor. Mostyn watched Beames try to block her ears, only to have her hands tied together so she couldn't. She sat, softly sobbing the entire time. Slezak's screaming was silenced by a gag. Mostyn saw Jones clenching and unclenching his fists and Zink appeared to be in a trance. Baker's muttered litany of epithets, probably learned in his Coast Guard days, provided a counterpoint to Kemper's.

At long last, the screaming from the amphitheater stopped and Ger-Hy'la-T'la led Mostyn and his people, surrounded by guards, to the huge hall circling the interior of the edifice, by the main floor entrance where Mostyn had originally entered. They were formed into a line with a guard between each of them and one on each end of the row. Slezak's gag was removed and Beames's hands were untied.

From out of a door came the horrific mutilations. Ger-Hy'la-T'la informed them their former compatriots were now *y'm-bhi* slaves. They had been reanimated into the live-dead. They would serve the K'n-yanians by forever guarding the tunnel to the surface world that Mostyn and his people had used to gain access to K'n-yan.

At the sight of the first mutilation, Slezak fainted and Kemper threw up, even though she was used to seeing bodies in all manner of decay and dismemberment. The thing was a pair of legs joined together where the hips should have been and two arms attached to where the legs were joined together.

Next was a long snake-like body with Patty Gibson's head attached, mouth still sewn shut. All Mostyn could think was the torturers had completely reassembled her body. Tanner's head was attached to a pair of hands, the fingers slowly pulling the monstrosity across the floor.

Another body was headless, and its arms and legs had been swapped, so the thing now walked on its hands. Yet another of the living dead had Eliza Pettigrew's head, shoulders, and arms directly attached to her hips. Her torso was missing.

The ghastly and grizzly parade continued to pass by and moved slowly out into the street until the last nauseous insane deformity disappeared out the door.

Mostyn heard Kemper mutter, "God, these bastards make the Ahnenerbe-SS look like kindergartners." And he couldn't have agreed more.

His team members were taken away one by one until Mostyn was the last one remaining. As Dotty Kemper was taken away, she told Mostyn she loved him and he replied, "And I you, Dot." He blew her a kiss.

The carriage ride back to Mostyn's room was a long, lonely journey even though there were the four mannikin guards and the jailer that Mostyn now hated with a passion he had never felt before. He did not look at the man and the K'n-yanian made no attempt to communicate with him.

Mostyn didn't know how he'd do it, but he was going to escape with the remainder of his people, and he hoped he had the chance to let at least a few of these immortal K'n-yanians experience death.

9

THE LAND of K'n-yan is constantly bathed in a bluish light. Consequently, there is no natural division into day and night. As near as Mostyn could tell, there seemed to be an arbitrary division of time into rest periods and activity periods which simulated the day and night of his own world. Perhaps this was an indication that the K'n-yanians had once lived on the surface of the planet. If he had the time, he might see if he could find out from the records of their history.

Stripped of his watch, he had no idea how long the cycles were, nor did it seem that the times of rest and activity were universally followed. After all, the K'n-yanians did no work. That was taken care of by slaves. At least, that is how it seemed to Mostyn from his limited observations.

When he'd gotten back to his room, he'd found guests waiting for him. Ten members of his affection group.

The table was filled with food and a second table had

been brought in and was filled with an assortment of bottles.

Four of the men and women were sitting, eating, drinking, and laughing. A slave was performing music on a type of harp and singing, a man and a woman were copulating in Mostyn's bed, and two other couples were dancing.

Mostyn, however, was in no mood for partying and asked them to leave. They didn't protest, although three of them seemed upset at being tossed out. Mostyn didn't care. He'd just witnessed the butchering of six good men and women. Men and women he was responsible for. As far as he was concerned, they could all go to hell. Or better yet, be lunch for Tsathaggua.

He was tired. Emotionally drained. He looked at his bed in disgust. He had no desire to sleep where two people had been getting his sheets wet with love juices. Instead he flopped down on the sofa.

His gaze rested on the tables. He got up and walked over to them. All manner of food and drink and he had no idea what any of it was. He filled a plate with whatever looked good and picked up a bottle. There was no stopper in it and he took a swig. Some type of wine. He would have preferred gin. But any port in a storm, as they say.

Back to the sofa he walked and stretched out on it, balancing the plate of food on his stomach. He took another swig of wine and ate something that looked like a cracker with a dollop of a salmon-colored paste on it.

"Whatever that was, it doesn't taste too bad," he said out loud.

He took another swig of wine and ate a slice of a blue-green veggie that had a chunk of something dark brown on it. Maybe roasted fungus. That too was pretty tasty.

If he had even briefly entertained a thought to stay in K'n-yan, today's event had put an end to it. He had to escape with his people. There was no doubt in his mind Bardon was planning some manner of rescue. But he couldn't wait for that. He had no idea if Bardon would be successful.

According to Langley's summary of Zamacona's journal, there were other tunnels and the K'n-yanians had closed them off. But what if they had missed some? Like the one Zamacona had discovered? There was, of course, the one they'd uncovered. It would be heavily guarded, yet it might be their only route to the surface. He needed to find out more about the country. He needed to learn the K'n-yan language so he could read. Or he needed a friend.

Until he knew otherwise, he had to entertain the possibility that there were other tunnels to the surface that were unknown and therefore unguarded. If it turned out there weren't, then he'd have to use the one he knew about. Guarded or not. He had to assume there was a way out.

He wanted to see Dotty more than a brief visit every two weeks. And he wanted to see the sun, the moon, the stars. Not this goddamn blue light. Shit. He didn't even like the color blue.

He finished the food on the plate and set it on the floor. Then he went to work on the bottle.

———

Running. Running with nowhere to hide. The hideous deformities that had been the soldiers assigned to protect his people were after him. And they were gaining on him because, being dead, they could never tire.

He turned a corner and ran down a deserted street. The blue light didn't reach everywhere and there were no street lights. In front of him, from out of the shadows, they appeared. Dozens of deformities.

A faceless head, attached to a limbless torso with a face on its stomach, yelled, "Traitor! Traitor!" Another monstrosity, a shapeless lump of flesh, with hands and feet and a mouth, asked, in Dotty Kemper's voice, "Why didn't you help us? Why didn't you save us?"

Mostyn stopped and turned to flee back down the way he came, only to see the rest of his team, all turned into *y'm-bhi* slaves, blocking his escape.

He turned around and the shapeless blob was in front of him. "Kiss me, Pierce. Kiss me." It demanded, in Dotty's voice.

Mostyn screamed. Hands were on him, shaking him.

"Mostyn Pierce, wake up! Wake up!"

He sat up, chest heaving. Staring him in the face wasn't a shapeless hunk of flesh that had once been Dotty Kemper. It was the beautiful and concerned face of H'tha-dub.

"Mostyn Pierce, it was only a dream," she said in Spanish. "You have no need to fear. You are awake and I am here."

He looked around the room. The curtain had been pulled across the window, which made the light in the room soft and diffused. Giving it a feeling of twilight. His eyes returned to H'tha-dub.

She sent her thoughts to him. "You were dreaming. You are okay." Her hand touched his face and Mostyn recoiled as though it were on fire.

In Spanish, she said, "It's me, H'tha-dub, Mostyn Pierce."

Mostyn replied in Spanish, "Get out! You barbarous bunch of barbaric savages! You tortured my people to death!"

He launched himself at her, got his hands on her neck, and they tumbled to the floor. He squeezed, his thumbs pushing in on her throat. However, she did not resist him. She simply lay there letting him strangle the life out of her.

When Mostyn realized she wasn't fighting him, he released his hold on her neck, and sat on the floor. H'tha-dub stretched out her hand to touch his arm and, before she could touch him, he jumped up and went to the window, pulling the curtains aside.

"I think you are hurt, Mostyn Pierce. But I did not hurt you. I only want you to pleasure me and give me new experiences and I want to do the same for you."

He turned around and faced her. "Were you there? Did you cheer?" he demanded.

"At the amphitheater?"

Mostyn nodded.

"No. I was not there."

On hearing her words, his attitude softened somewhat, and seeing that, she said, "Let me comfort you, Mostyn Pierce. Let me take away the hurt."

"You can't. You can't take away the hurt."

She came up to him and hugged him. Holding him and gently rocking him side to side. After a few moments, Mostyn put his arms around her waist.

"Why me?" he asked. "Why are you interested in me?"

"You remind me of Pánfilo. Yet you are different. I loved Pánfilo and wanted him for myself. Instead he chose T'la-yub, only because she could help him escape. I felt such intense pain at his rejection. It was a new experience to hurt so. And yet I did not like it. I received permission to go to another affection group, as I could no longer endure the pain of even seeing Pánfilo. In the end, her *y'm-bhi* turned him over to the guards. She no longer knew who he was."

"I'm sorry, H'tha-dub, for you having to experience his rejection. But don't I cause you pain if I remind you of him?"

"You remind me of Pánfilo, and yet you are different from him." She pulled away and held Mostyn at arm's length. "You have… I don't know the Spanish." She looked into his eyes and Mostyn heard in his mind, "You have strength of character. You are a man of strong will. And that is new and exciting. The men here do not possess these qualities and I am filled with desire to know them and have them all to myself."

Mostyn didn't know quite how to respond and settled for, "I'll take that as a compliment."

"That was my intent, Mostyn Pierce." She took him by the hand and led him to the table, chose a morsel of food and held it up to his mouth. After a moment's hesitation he opened his mouth and she fed him.

"Pánfilo spoke of a thing he called marriage. It is where in your world a man and a woman make their own affection group and have children. He said that when children come, it is called a family. He told T'la-yub he would do marriage with her when they escaped."

Mostyn looked at H'tha-dub and had a sinking feeling in his gut.

"I know you want to go back to your world. If you will do this marriage with me and take me with you to the upper world, I will try to help you escape."

"H'tha-dub, I, I..." He looked at her and the words stuck in his throat. He closed his eyes. Dotty. Dotty's face filled his mind.

Her voice, speaking Spanish, came to his ears, "You must make me your affection group, Mostyn Pierce, now. If you don't, I will go away and you will remain here until you die."

10

MOSTYN WAS DUMBSTRUCK. He opened his eyes and turned away from H'tha-dub.

Dotty. He loved Dotty.

But to get his people out of the hell they were in, he'd have to commit himself to this woman. This K'n-yanian. He could tell her no. Or he could try to reason with her and explain to her his commitment to Dotty as the reason why he couldn't make the commitment she asked of him. He could do that. And what would her response be? He swallowed down a bitter chuckle. She would be gone in a flash. She wanted no more heartaches such as Pánfilo had given her. And without H'tha-dub, what were the chances of getting anyone else to help him? What were the chances of him being able to escape by himself, let alone with the rest of his team? The answer to the latter questions was simple: he stood no chance.

As for finding someone else to help? The odds were very good everyone knew of Zamacona and T'la-yub. Their escape attempt, their capture, and her subsequent mutilation, decapitation, and reanimation as a *y'm-bhi* sent to warn forever the surface dwellers away from the gate in the mound.

And everyone undoubtedly knew of Zamacona's second escape attempt, his capture by T'la-yub, and of his death by mutilation and his own reanimation as a *y'm-bhi* guard of the very passageway through which he'd sought his escape.

All that told Mostyn his chance of finding anyone to help him was next to zero. Who would want to risk being mutilated to death just to help a bunch of surface dwellers go home? People, whose death by mutilation might provide some rip-roaringly good entertainment?

Mostyn shook his head. No, the odds weren't next to zero. They were less than zero.

He turned back to face her. She was standing as he'd left her. Watching him. What if this were a trick? A test. What if she was an agent of the chief executive? What if the K'n-yanians wanted an excuse, any excuse to get rid of Mostyn and his people?

She seemed devoid of guile. Then again, the same could probably be said of Mata Hari, Anna Chapman, and Belle Boyd. Yet, what choice did he have? He was going to make an escape attempt sooner or later — especially if Bardon was unable to mount a rescue attempt. He would either succeed or he wouldn't. If H'tha-dub could help him, so much the better. If she betrayed him, he wouldn't be any worse off since the chance of an escape attempt succeeding was nil.

Mostyn looked her in the eyes and sent his thoughts to

her. "I will do as you ask, but only if all of my people leave with us."

Now it was H'tha-dub's turn to contemplate the situation, but she did not take long. "If you will be my affection partner, then I will do as you ask so all of the surface dwellers can go home."

"Thank you, H'tha-dub."

She came to him and kissed him, her arms around his neck, her tongue probing his mouth. Mostyn tried to reply in kind, but his heart wasn't in it.

H'tha-dub was beautiful. Alabaster skin, hair that was as dark as a moonless night, the high cheekbones, slender Aquiline nose, and those thin yet shapely lips. The scent she wore was intoxicating.

Yet all he could think of was Dotty and, because of Dotty, Mostyn had no heart for this woman kissing him. Under other circumstances he would have felt himself lucky to be with her. Unfortunately, those other circumstances did not exist and Mostyn hated himself for having to deceive this woman to get what he wanted.

She broke the kiss and reached behind her back. The gold belt fell to the floor and her robe followed.

"Come, Mostyn Pierce." She took his hand and pulled him towards the bed.

He followed. His steps wooden. When they reached the foot of the bed, she let go of his hand, and lay upon the sheets.

"Come, Mostyn Pierce. Come to me. Let us now become one flesh."

Mostyn felt sick. The soft breaths of H'tha-dub touched his back. She was fast asleep. The sex had been exquisite, but Dotty's face was ever before him and in the end he did not enjoy it. He'd done his best to pretend he was interested, and if H'tha-dub had any suspicions she'd said nothing. Several times in the midst of her ecstasy she'd cried out in her native language and always in the middle of the unknown words was "Mostyn Pierce".

He got out of bed and walked to the window. No stars. Just the distant vaulted ceiling of stone and that hated blue light. No one was about on the street. It must be the rest period.

Dotty. Would she understand he'd betrayed her to free her and the others? Would she forgive him? In all honesty, Mostyn doubted she would. Dotty Kemper was hard as nails. Yet under that shell, she was soft and feminine and wanted to be loved and cared for. She wanted sweet nothings whispered in her ear and little butterfly kisses trailed down her back.

"Oh, God, what have I done?" The words came out freighted with despair.

He felt arms encircle his waist, and soft skin and hair against his left shoulder.

"What did you say, Mostyn Pierce?" The words were Spanish.

"I said I miss the stars."

"I long to see them with you, Mostyn Pierce. Little dots of white light in a black expanse. Is that not so?"

"Yes."

"Such a new experience! The longing to see them gives me such joy and pain. The pain of longing and the joy of anticipation. Oh, Mostyn Pierce…" She turned him around to face her and lay her head on his chest. "I like this feeling I have. It is new and exciting and I never want it to go away. I am very happy we have done this thing called marriage. I have never experienced such joy. And to think I almost went into *km'bha*."

"What is *km'bha?*"

"It is a semi-spectral state some of us resort to when there is no more pleasure to be found in this life. Others resort to death when no more pleasure is to be found. You have given me back to life, Mostyn Pierce."

"But what of the upper world? I will grow old and die. You can live forever, am I right?"

"If I so choose, I can become young again. I am over nine hundred years old."

Mostyn lifted her face. She looked no more than perhaps twenty-five. "H'tha-dub, what will you do when I'm old and feeble? When I die?"

"I will grow old and feeble with you and I will die with you, Mostyn Pierce."

"And you're sure this is what you want?"

"Yes, Mostyn Pierce. This is what I want. Now come. Let us be… What did Pánfilo say?"

"Husband and wife?"

"Oh, yes! That is it! Come to me, my love. Let us be husband and wife."

She was beautiful, this woman of an unknown and in so many ways superior race of human beings. Yet Mostyn could only think of Dotty and that even if they did escape, he'd lost everything worth living for.

11

When Mostyn woke, H'tha-dub was gone. He got out of bed, padded over to the bathroom and decided to take a bath. He looked in the mirror. He needed a shave. The K'n-yanian males had no mustaches or beards. Did they shave? Or didn't they have facial hair? He'd have to inquire about getting a razor. He also needed to find out how many days had passed since coming to K'n-yan.

The bath water was warm and while Mostyn preferred a shower, he found the bath relaxing. One thing that puzzled him was why there had been no attempt so far by the OUP to rescue them. At least no attempt that he'd been made aware of. Maybe there had been and he was being kept in the dark about it. Which would make a lot of sense from the viewpoint of the K'n-yanians. Maybe H'tha-dub could find out for him.

At the thought of her, a great sadness came over him. If she did go with him to the surface, the OUP would latch onto her like Blackbeard onto a treasure ship. He would lose her and Dotty both. What a mess. What a goddamn mess.

He held his nose and slid under the water. For about twenty seconds he stayed there under the surface of the water and then sat up.

"Stop feeling sorry for yourself, Mostyn," he said out loud. "Your personal life has nothing to do with this mission. You have yourself and six other people to get out of here and back to the land of sun, moon, and stars. Your duty, mister, comes first. If you have to deceive H'tha-dub and cheat on Dotty in order to save six people, then that's what you have to do. Because those six lives are what's important. Not even your own life is as important as theirs. That's the nature of this job, and you accepted it. Voluntarily. This mission is no different than any other."

He got out of the tub, toweled off, and put on his robe. Another look in the mirror convinced him he needed a shave, and then he walked out of the bathroom.

H'tha-dub was not around and someone had cleared the table, taken the second table away, and left breakfast. Along with a new chair to replace the one he'd broken.

He sat at the table and began eating. The food was good, whatever it was. The beverage was some kind of fruit juice and tasted something like blueberries. There was meat on the plate and, like last time, he left it untouched.

Giving his situation some thought, he needed quite a bit of information. He'd have to find out how much H'tha-dub knew, and what she didn't know he'd have to pick her brain as to the best way to get the answers he needed.

He needed to know what "day" it was. That is, how

many days he had been in K'n-yan. Had Bardon made one or more rescue attempts? Where were his teammates being housed? And where was their equipment? They needed as much firepower as they could muster. For one, he didn't remember hearing the machine gun firing. Which meant they had a potent weapon at their disposal, if they could get to it. There were the grenades, too. They could be a big help in slowing down any pursuing K'n-yanians. If they could get hold of their things, they would have a better chance at escaping.

Mostyn also needed to know where the tunnel was by which they entered K'n-yan in relation to the city, and the best route to it. And if there were any other tunnels by which they might escape.

Mulling over the list of information he needed, Mostyn quickly realized his dependence on H'tha-dub. There was no way he'd be able to get any of the information on his own. At least not without spending years learning the K'n-yanian world as had Zamacona. And the K'n-yanians, having dealt with the Spaniard, would be wary in talking with him, would be on their guard to not give him anything he might use to mount an escape attempt. All the while, of course, trying to get data from him about the upper world. Which was why he had implemented Plan Epsilon. Be cooperative, yet give them nothing, and find out how to escape. If escape plans could be shared, share them. Otherwise, escape on your own.

The one advantage Mostyn had, as he saw it, was that he was not confined to the room. He and H'tha-dub could move about freely. He'd be able to use the relative freedom of movement to collect valuable data. And that gave him hope.

Breakfast finished, he left the table and went over to the window. From behind him, in Spanish, he heard, "You are always at that window, Mostyn Pierce. You look like a caged *g'n-da* longing for freedom."

He turned around. "Where I'm from, we'd say a caged bird. Do you have birds here? Creatures that fly through the air? And sing pretty songs?"

"We do. However, we do not cage them. For then they cease to sing."

"They must not take well to prison. Like people."

"I suppose not," she said.

Mostyn's eyes swept the figure of H'tha-dub from her face to her feet. Her robe had a diamond-shaped cut from just below the collar to where her belt encircled her waist. God, she was beautiful. If it weren't for the feelings he had for Dotty... He noticed she'd applied a light touch of makeup and looked even more ravishing than normal. The scent of her perfume wafted to him. Floral, with undertones of moss and musk.

Conflicting emotions of desire and regret seized him and he pushed them away. He had a duty to his team. She was expendable, as even he was expendable. She was a tool, he told himself. A tool to secure his team's escape.

He opened his arms and smiled at her. She ran to him, embracing and kissing him.

"Where were you?" he asked, in Spanish.

"I went to see the *gn'agn*."

"What's that?"

"I don't know the words."

She looked into his eyes and Mostyn understood the term to mean the supreme tribunal of Tsath.

"And why did you wish to see them?" he asked, once again using Spanish.

"I wanted permission to be your watcher. You and the others are under a suspended death penalty. If you give the people of K'n-yan the slightest reason to do so, your stay of execution will be lifted and you will be mutilated in the most colorful and entertaining manner imaginable."

Mostyn didn't find that information very encouraging. "What did they say?"

"They agreed to transfer you to my apartment and to my care, with the understanding that if the need arises to execute you, I will be executed as well."

"How did you persuade them?"

"I told them men from the upper world are very suscep-tible to manipulation by women. There is, of course, the situation with Pánfilo and T'la-yub and the one in your group called 'Jones'."

Mostyn shook his head. Leave it to Jones, he thought, to screw things up. God's gift to women.

"However, Ger-Hy'la-T'la will be present when you meet with your people and with our learned ones."

"Why not you?"

"One of the *gn'agn* expressed concern that you might be persuasive as was Pánfilo. And so Ger-Hy'la-T'la will be with you when you talk to your people and to those of my people who are in authority. Come, Mostyn Pierce. I take you to your new home. The home of your wife."

"What about the affection group?"

"What about them?"

"Won't they be angry?"

"Angry? No. Why should they be? They will visit and we will enjoy their companionship and then they will leave. We will simply not have sex with them."

"How convenient." Mostyn muttered in English.

"Are you okay, Mostyn Pierce?"

"I'm fine, beautiful one."

H'tha-dub's face lit up at the term of endearment. "Oh, Mostyn Pierce, my love, I am so glad you came to our world and I am so very happy we are going to yours. Come now, your new bed awaits your warmth."

12

HE'D LEARNED from H'tha-dub that the day he moved to her suite was day four that he and his team were in K'n-yan. Day one being the day of capture. A day being one activity period and one rest period. The K'n-yanian method of telling time wasn't much different than that of his world, Mostyn realized. The time of rest ended the day. And as with many Americans, the rest period, or night, didn't necessarily mean people actually rested. K'n-yanians tended to party through most of the rest period and sleep through most of the activity period.

And since K'n-yanians had no need to work, there being an overabundance of slaves and machinery to do that for them, Mostyn learned the hard way that trying to motivate H'tha-dub to the task of leaving was tantamount to trying to push a two-ton truck uphill with the parking brake on.

The semi-anarchistic nature of K'n-yanian society meant habit tended to be the prime motivator to action. The typical day for K'n-yanians consisted of playing games, getting drunk, participating in sexual and gastronomic orgies, torturing slaves for entertainment, sitting around daydreaming, discussing art and philosophy, participating in religious ceremonies (often orgiastic in nature), and anything else the mind could come up with that didn't involve work.

In this, H'tha-dub was no different than any other member of her race. She wanted to play and, in her particular case, to spend the day in bed copulating with Mostyn. Something he chalked up to being akin to a child's fascination with a new toy. In many ways, he saw the K'n-yanians as very childlike in their approach to life.

After two days of eating, drinking, sex, playing a game somewhat similar to backgammon, and visiting with members of their affection group, Mostyn finally got H'tha-dub to agree to go out with him and to gather the information that he needed.

For this day, day seven of his being in K'n-yan, Mostyn wanted to get some familiarity with the city. He needed to know how it was laid out, and what were the ways into and out of it. To that end, he and H'tha-dub spent what he figured were two or three hours walking up and down the various streets. People were about, none in a hurry. There were no street vendors, no street musicians, no homeless people, no storefronts, no factories, no vehicles. Mostyn asked H'tha-dub about this.

"The slaves do all our work. If I want a new robe, I order one of my slaves to make it. My slaves tend my garden and my animals. If I need to buy something, which does not happen very often at all, I pay the owner of a slave who can make whatever it is I need. But seriously, Mostyn Pierce, what do I need?"

"You have a point. You seem to have everything."

"We K'n-yanians don't travel much and haven't for many centuries. Therefore, we have little need of vehicles. Slaves grow our food and make our wine, repair our dwellings, make our clothes, and build our furniture. There is no need for factories or shops. Anything we need is made for us. We own very little. Even the Tulu metal, which we value and hold to be sacred, was distributed equally to all K'n-yanians. Over the centuries, some have acquired more to the loss of others. But no one is without the metal, everyone has some, and no one is without any of the necessities of life."

Mostyn thought for a moment on what she said before speaking. "Are you happy?"

"I am now."

"You weren't before?"

"No, not before. I was tired of life. Tired of doing the same things with the same people every day for hundreds of years."

Almost to himself, Mostyn muttered, "So utopia has its price and it's called boredom."

"I do not understand. What is 'utopia'?"

"More or less what you have here. No problems, no worries. Everyone has everything they could possibly need — except happiness."

H'tha-dub seemed to ruminate on his words for a moment, before replying. "Yes, I think this is true what you say. Do you in your world have everything you want?"

"Far from it. Most of us work, and work hard, and don't get anywhere near what we want. Many don't even get what they need."

H'tha-dub stopped walking and turned to Mostyn. "You work? Don't you have slaves?"

"Nope. No slaves. I have to do the work I need done, or pay someone else to do the work, or buy a machine to do it. And the money to pay the person or buy the machine comes from the job I have to go to five, or more, days a week."

"A job? What is this 'job'?"

"It's work I do that I get money for doing."

"I don't understand. Do you mean to say I must become a slave when I go to your world? But I'll be a slave that gets money for what slaves are just supposed to do?"

"Something like that."

She started walking again, and Mostyn walked with her.

"What a strange world you live in, Mostyn Pierce."

"You still want to go there?"

She stopped and turned to him. "Yes, Mostyn Pierce. I want this new experience to be a slave who gets money for working." Then she clapped her hands like a little child and a big smile broke out on her face. "I could live forever on all the new experiences of your world!"

"Except I wouldn't be there with you."

Suddenly her face became sad. "No, you would not. How long will you live, Mostyn Pierce?"

"Maybe another forty or fifty years."

"Oh, no! That few?"

"Yes, that few."

She turned and started walking, her pace slow. Mostyn had no trouble keeping up with her. She said nothing. He looked at the profile of her face. A tear slowly rolled down her cheek.

"Still want to come to my world?"

"Yes, Mostyn Pierce. At least my days will end with me being happy and wanting more. I think that will be much better than being tired and bored."

Mostyn hoped she'd still feel that way when actually facing death, knowing there was still so much to live for and that she'd never get to experience it. Everyone he knew who had died had done so filled with regret. Regret for having missed or not taken advantage of the many chances to do and to enjoy.

Having walked through a large section of the city, they chose a path that led to the grassy area surrounding Tsath.

"Do you know where the tunnel entrance is that leads back up to my world?"

"The one by which you came here?"

"Yes."

"No. I will do my best to find out."

"Do you know of any other tunnels to the surface?"

"I do not. There are old books in the library. Perhaps they contain the information you seek."

Mostyn wasn't happy with the answer she gave him. There was no concept of the notion of urgency. He took a deep breath. He was not dealing with a person from his world. She was a K'n-yanian. She lived in an isolated and static world. A world that had stopped growing. She'd probably learned all that was needed to be learned centuries ago. She was in charge of nothing. Her day consisted of nothing but one long exercise in hedonistic pleasure-seeking. And even children and teenagers get bored. A person reaches a point where no new pleasures can be thought of because one has exhausted one's pool of knowledge.

What a dismal world to live in. No wonder she was excited to be with him and wanted to leave K'n-yan for his world, Mostyn thought. The risk of a hideous death was worth the attempt to escape the stultifying and death-odored boredom of her life. He'd just have to figure out a way to light a fire under her butt to get her moving.

"H'tha-dub?"

"Yes, Mostyn Pierce?"

He barely suppressed a laugh. Her eyes and face made him think of a puppy filled with anticipation as to what her master was going to say or do next. "If you want to help me get to my world—"

"I do, Mostyn Pierce, because I know this is a very important thing to you who come from the world above. You are like the *dor'tlin* that must always return to the same cliff to mate and bear their young. You will never be satisfied living in my world and will even suffer the amphitheater just as long as you get the chance to make an attempt to escape. It was so with Pánfilo and I know it will be so with you."

"You are right. That is how it is with us from the world above. Therefore, we must work quickly. Time is very important. The longer I and my people are here, the more difficult it will be for us to escape."

"Tell me what I must do. I shall try to be a slave. Yes! I'll pretend I am a slave and you are my master and I must do your bidding. Tell me, oh my master, what I must do."

Mostyn did everything he could to not burst out laughing. Never in a million years could he have imagined this scene ever taking place. He took a deep breath and repeated the things he needed to know before he could do any more planning. H'tha-dub responded by telling him she'd get the information to him as speedily as was humanly possible.

While they walked and talked in the grassy park surrounding the city, Mostyn carefully observed every detail. Nothing at this point was extraneous information. Everything was important. Like, for example, the repulsively horned *gyaa-yothn* he saw scattered throughout the grassy park. Their rudimentary intelligence was undoubtedly sufficient to make them reliable observers. And that they were observing him, he had no doubt.

The park was about a mile wide. Farm fields lay beyond it, according to H'tha-dub. There were a few trees in the wide expanse of the grass. Mostly, though, the land was open. A giant meadow. The park was considered common land, she told him. Privately held lands were beyond.

When they returned to H'tha-dub's apartment, they were visited by members of their affection group and the afternoon vanished in eating and drinking, dematerializations, discussions over the purpose of life, and speculations as to whether any of the upper worlders would be able to live beyond one hundred years.

Mostyn, his mind on other things, found the afternoon

a waste of time. Twice he was approached by members of the group asking if he'd have sex with them. He politely turned each one down. When one woman became insistent, he told her he found her repulsive-looking, and that put an end to her advancements.

When the last of the affection group departed, to continue the party elsewhere, Mostyn asked to be taken to the library. H'tha-dub protested, wanting to enjoy the pleasures of the bed with her own private affection group. Mostyn, however, prevailed and they set off for the central city. Once they got to the building housing the library of the great city of Tsath, he hoped she was up to the task of translating old books for him. Otherwise, he had a feeling he might be staying in K'n-yan a lot longer than he wanted.

13
―――――

THE NEXT MORNING did not start well for Mostyn. After the slave took away the breakfast dishes, H'tha-dub wanted to play in bed and Mostyn got short with her.

"I am not spending the rest of my life in this hell hole!" he mentally shouted at her. "You have to get that information for me and I need to review the notes I made from last night."

"But Mostyn Pierce—"

"Now! Get me that information! If you don't, I'm going to die a lot sooner than in forty or fifty years."

"I don't understand."

"If you don't get your butt out that door, I'm going to go on my own and—"

"Oh, no, Mostyn Pierce!" She threw her arms around him, kissed him, and dematerialized.

Mostyn walked over to the drawer in his wardrobe where he'd put his notes and the maps they'd taken from the library, although stolen might be a touch more accurate. He took out the sheaf of notes he'd written with a dip pen, using the liquid green ink the K'n-yanians favored. On seeing the antique writing implements, he'd expressed amazement that such an advanced people hadn't invented the ballpoint pen.

H'tha-dub didn't see the need for such an invention, since few of her people bothered to do any writing. And hadn't for at least five or six centuries. "I certainly haven't," she quipped.

To which, he'd replied, "Try it. It'll a be a new experience." And that made her eyes light up.

He settled on the couch only to hear a knock at the door. In K'n-yanian, he shouted, "Go away!"

The past few days hadn't all been spent screwing around. Mostyn had gotten H'tha-dub to teach him basic K'n-yanian words and phrases.

His tone of voice, however, did nothing to chase away the visitor. For a moment later Ger-Hy'la-T'la materialized in front of him.

Mostyn sent a blistering wave of thoughts to the K'n-yanian, and in return he asked the reason for Mostyn's hostility.

"I think you know why," Mostyn thought back. "Let me mutilate your affection group and see how you feel about it."

The K'n-yanian's face remained impassive. "We did not ask you to come here. Now come with me. It is time for your first interview with one of your people."

"It's about time. I was wondering how long it would

take for you people to get your collective act together. Who's the lucky person?"

"The one who is named Doctor Candy Slezak."

A feeling of relief passed over Mostyn. He wasn't ready to face Dotty, and seeing Slezak would give him the opportunity to see how she was holding up, being, in his estimation, the weak link on his team.

"Give me a minute," was the thought Mostyn sent to the K'n-yanian. He got off the couch, set the thin vellum sheets aside, and went looking for his sandals.

When he came back to the living room, he found Ger-Hy'la-T'la holding the papers and looking at them. Mostyn walked up to him and snatched them out of his hand.

In Spanish, knowing the language was something of an irritant to the K'n-yanian leaders, he said, "Where I come from, what you did just now is considered rude."

Ger-Hy'la-T'la bowed, and in Spanish replied, "Please accept my apology. I was curious. Writing is something of a novelty, since few of us write anything anymore."

Mostyn thought to himself, thank God the words were in English. To the K'n-yanian, he sent his thoughts, "Too bad. Writing is a wonderful experience."

Ger-Hy'la-T'la raised his eyebrows in response. "I may have to try it again. Follow me."

Mostyn followed him out of the apartment and out to the street. They walked several blocks and then turned into another building, took the stairs to the second floor, walked down a hallway, and turned into another apartment. Once inside, Mostyn saw a female K'n-yanian and Candy Slezak.

When Slezak saw him, she said, "Hi, Pierce!"

And he greeted her in return. Although to his ears her voice had an odd quality to it.

Ger-Hy'la-T'la informed Mostyn the apartment was his home. The woman was from Slezak's affection group and was her escort, her name being N'ga-yub.

Mostyn replied he'd like to speak with Slezak alone.

"That is not possible," Ger-Hy'la-T'la replied. "However, since you will speak in your own language, we won't be able to understand you."

"Very well," Mostyn conceded. He turned to his teammate. "How are they treating you, Candy?"

"Wonderfully!" she replied. "My affection group is so nice. They took me in right away. It's been nothing but party central."

Mostyn looked at her eyes. The pupils were mere pinpoints. "Are you high?" he asked.

"Man, they have the best shit here. Pierce, if we could take this stuff home we'd be millionaires overnight. I haven't been straight for days. And these people are so horny. My God, I'm so fucked out."

"Slezak. This is a new experience for them. Once they get used to you, things will change. You'll just become the same old stuff."

"Stuffy ol' Pierce Mostyn. You need to lighten up, man."

"Plan Epsilon, Slezak."

"I don't know, Pierce. I didn't want to come here and you made me. Now that I'm here, I kind of like it. I don't think I want to go back."

"Listen to me, Candy. You have family and friends. You have your work."

"You know what, Pierce? There's no work here." She leaned forward and spoke in almost a whisper. "They don't worry about money, or disease, or loneliness. Nothing. It's a perfect world here. And I'm learning their language. Although with all the fucking..." She started giggling. "It doesn't leave time for much else." Her voice trailed off into a fit of laughter.

"Candy. Listen to me. I need your help. We all need your help to get out of here. We have to work together."

"Well, Pierce, Mr Mostyn, sir, I'm not sure I want to help. I kind of like it here." She stood, spoke something in K'n-yanian to N'ga-yub, and then turned back to Mostyn.

"See you around, Pierce. I'm going to a worship service with my affection group. Sounds like a lot more fucking. Bye!" She wiggled her fingers at Mostyn and left with N'ga-yub.

"Things did not go to your satisfaction, Mostyn?"

He turned and noticed Ger-Hy'la-T'la looking at him. "Oh, everything is just peachy," he thought back.

"You have such strange expressions. Come, I will take you back to H'tha-dub's apartment."

On the way back, Mostyn said nothing. This was not good. How were the others holding up? Or were they? Had they, too, given in to K'n-yanian hedonism?

When he closed the door behind him at H'tha-dub's place, out of his peripheral vision he saw a shape running towards him. His reflexes kicked in. He dropped, rolled, and was on his feet just in time to watch H'tha-dub land in a heap on the floor.

Mostyn went to her and kneeled beside her. "I'm so terribly sorry," he said in Spanish. "I just reacted. Are you all right?"

"Oh, Mostyn Pierce!" she exclaimed through her sobs. "I came back and you were not here. I thought you were so angry with me that you left."

He held her in his arms. "No, I didn't leave." He then explained why he'd been gone from the apartment.

"I love you, Mostyn Pierce. Please don't scare me again."

"I won't. At least not intentionally."

"I did what you asked, and I think you will be very happy with me, Mostyn Pierce. Very happy."

14

MOSTYN WAS INDEED VERY happy with the information H'tha-dub had gotten for him. How she'd gotten it and from whom, she hadn't said and Mostyn hadn't asked. His only concern was if it was reliable.

"Oh, yes, Mostyn Pierce. The information is as reliable as the blue light which is always present."

And that was good enough for him. From the floor, they'd moved to the sofa and sitting together she'd told him all she knew.

Twice, soldiers from the upper world had tried to force their way through the tunnel and both times the K'n-yanian slaves and *y'm-bhi* had turned back the top-worlders.

"And to celebrate our victories," H'tha-dub said, "four of the slain warriors from your world were turned into *y'm-bhi* to guard the tunnel."

This news distressed Mostyn. Not only had Bardon underestimated the K'n-yanians, but the K'n-yanians had taken to gloating over their victories and he hoped that wouldn't have ramifications for him and his people.

She went on to tell him what he'd been secretly fearing. "There are rumors the Council of Executives want to seal the tunnel through which you came to our world."

"It's a logical move," he'd replied. "I'm surprised they haven't done so already."

"I know where the tunnel is. A gate has been put across the entrance and there are guards, but we can get through."

"That is just about the only good news, but it is good news. Wonderfully good news, as a matter of fact."

H'tha-dub was ecstatic she'd pleased Mostyn. "But there's more, Mostyn Pierce."

"Let's hear it, then."

"All the tunnels to your world are closed. The only one now open is the one you opened."

Mostyn nodded. "Which means our only escape route is our best escape route."

H'tha-dub continued. "I've located all of your people, except for the one called 'Candy' and the one called 'DC'. Your equipment is in an abandoned temple devoted to the worship of Tsathoggua."

"Do you know where it is?"

"Yes. It is a short journey outside of the city."

"Why are they being kept there?"

"So no one will touch them. We do not enter the temples of Tsathoggua. He is a very dangerous god."

"So I've heard."

"You know of Tsathoggua?"

"Yes. Are there guards?"

"No. There is no need. No one from this world would enter the place."

"Even better."

"Have I done well, Mostyn Pierce?"

"You have done exceedingly well, my sweet, sweet flower."

"My love." Her hand touched his face. "Do you want me to remove the prickles?"

"You have a razor?"

"No. What is it?"

Mostyn thought a moment. "A razor is something like a knife, only it's used to remove hair."

She laughed. "We have no need for such a thing. I will show you." She put her hands on his face and closed her eyes. After a few moments, she opened them and removed her hands.

"All gone," she announced.

"What?" Mostyn got up and went to the bathroom. When he came back, he sat and asked, "How did you do that?"

"I dematerialized them."

"Well, I'll be damned. Sure as hell wish I could bottle *that*."

She giggled. "I made you happy, didn't I?"

"You sure did."

"Oh, Mostyn Pierce!" She jumped up, kneeled on the floor before him, and putting her arms around him, gave him a kiss.

Laying her head in his lap, she said, "What a wonderful new experience is this making someone happy."

In some ways, she's just a child, he thought. Naïve. Innocent. And yet... His mind went back to the amphitheater and the delight that her fellow K'n-yanians took in the torturing and killing of others. Worse than Rome's barbarism. This people, H'tha-dub included, were far from being naïve and innocent.

"H'tha-dub?"

"Yes, my darling one?"

"Can your people talk to each other without looking at each other?"

"Oh, yes, Mostyn Pierce. It is a simple act of the will. If I want you to hear me, you do. And if you want me to hear you, I will. It's just easier for beginners like yourself to focus by looking into someone's eyes."

"Why didn't anyone tell me about this?"

"I guess no one thought to do so. We have so very few who must learn to throw their thoughts. I think Pánfilo was the last one."

Mostyn absorbed what H'tha-dub had told him. The information cleared up the mystery as to how Ger-Hy'la-T'la had spoken to him even though he wasn't looking at him. Quite an ability.

"Can you read my thoughts?"

"Oh, no, Mostyn Pierce. I cannot look into your mind. I can only will my thoughts to you. I cannot experience your thoughts if you did not will for me to receive them."

Mostyn breathed a sigh of relief. That was a vital piece of information she'd given him. The K'n-yanians weren't mind readers. He could continue learning the language and teaching English to H'tha-dub and not have to worry about someone eavesdropping in his mind. Or hers, for that matter.

"All right, little flower, enough huggy time. We have work to do."

"We do? Why can't we stay here and be husband and wife?"

"Because I need to see where the tunnel is located."

"Do we have to go now?"

"Yes. We'll be more conspicuous during the rest period."

H'tha-dub let out a sigh. "Very well. For you, Mostyn Pierce, my love, for you, I'll take you there."

"Don't you want to come to my world? See the stars and the moon? Enjoy all the new experiences?"

Her face brightened and her eyes lit up. "Oh, yes, Mostyn Pierce, I do! Come, I'll show you. And then we can be husband and wife?"

Mostyn plastered a smile on his face. "Yes. Then we can be husband and wife."

15

H'THA-DUB LED Mostyn out of the city by a different route than she'd taken him the previous day.

This time, instead of walking, they rode on the *gyaa-yothn*, those hideously deformed abhuman creatures. Shockingly morbid, the great floundering black-haired beasts of burden were as universal in K'n-yan as horses were in nineteenth century America and Europe. Although the *gyaa-yothn* were far more docile and much more intelligent. In fact, they were dangerously intelligent. They'd been a key cause in Zamacona's failed escape attempt.

Mostyn had looked over his creature before mounting it. There was a decidedly human aspect to its bestiality, in spite of the rudimentary horn that projected from the forehead of its pug-like face. The hands and feet on which the creatures walked or ran were especially humanlike. They were also carnivores, eating the same flesh as the K'n-yanians. Namely, that sub-human slave class specially bred for food. He'd shuddered before climbing onto the creature.

He put aside his revulsion for the thing on which he sat and focused on the route H'tha-dub took through the mostly empty city streets. It was important he commit the way to the tunnel to memory. Just in case she wasn't around and he needed to leave.

The subterranean metropolis was immense. Its scope rivaled that of any great city on the surface. What was surprising to Mostyn was the lack of people and he asked H'tha-dub about it.

"There used to be many more of us. However, since we can live forever, there is little need for us to increase our numbers. Therefore, few children are born. Less than ten a year. If that many."

"Don't any of you die?"

"Yes. Some voluntarily. More because they committed some crime against our race."

"What do you mean?"

"We K'n-yanians are descended from the original worshipers the Great Old Ones brought with them to this world. In time, we encountered other people and enslaved them. And over the millennia many of those people regained their freedom. They are the freemen. They are not of us, but live with us. They are not K'n-yanians by blood."

"Don't they look like you?"

"Yes, for the most part. But they are not of us and are not to mingle with us. They live a long time, but not forever."

"So how many true K'n-yanians are there?"

"I do not know, Mostyn Pierce. We do not count our

numbers. Thousands to be sure. But I do not know the exact number."

"Who did my team encounter in the tunnels?"

"Probably *y'm-bhi*, slaves, and freemen."

Mostyn filed the information away. If the K'n-yanian defense force was composed of no K'n-yanians, just those living-dead beings, sub-human slaves, and freeman, then it might be possible to find a weak link among the freemen. If he could do so, his escape plan would have a much better chance of succeeding. How to find that weak link was the question.

Out of the city they rode, across the park, and into the countryside. The terrain here was rough and not suitable for farming. Not suitable for anything really. Rocky and with little soil to support plant growth.

The road on which they traveled was in a general state of disrepair, indicating it hadn't been used for a long time. That it was still usable indicated it had been built well. Like those old Roman roads still being used in Europe.

Mostyn looked at his wrist and silently cursed the K'n-yanians for taking his watch. He wasn't sure how long they'd been traveling. He guessed perhaps an hour, and certainly no more than that. Which meant, to his mind, they'd need eight of the *gyaa-yothn* and run them as fast as they could to have a chance at making their escape before the alarm was sounded.

"How much further?" he asked.

"I am not sure. I am not good at judging distances, Mostyn Pierce. The opening is a short distance past that rise."

"So this road goes right there?"

"Yes it does."

Mostyn nodded in response. That explained why it had fallen into disuse. Once the tunnel had been closed, there was no longer a need for the road. He wondered if that was the case with other abandoned roads. He'd have to look at the maps they found in the library and then check each one out, if he decided they needed to find an alternative route. Of course, trying to reopen a tunnel would be no small feat.

When they crested the rise, Mostyn signaled for H'tha-dub to stop. She reined in her *gyaa-yothn*. In the distance, Mostyn guessed no more than half a mile away, was a steep rock face that ascended up and up until it met the vast vaulted ceiling of stone far above them. And partway up the wall of rock, at that distance Mostyn couldn't tell how far, was an opening.

"That's the tunnel?"

"Yes, Mostyn Pierce. That is the path to your world."

"Let's get closer."

"I do not think that is wise."

"Why not?"

"There are guards."

"Precisely. I want to see how many and what they are."

Mostyn nudged his creature foreword and together he and H'tha-dub closed the gap until they were about fifteen hundred feet away.

There, in front of the gated opening in the cliff face, he saw six hideously deformed *y'm-bhi* slaves guarding the entrance into the tunnel. How do you kill something that's already dead? Mostyn asked himself. The flamethrower had worked beautifully, but that was no longer an option. All he could think of was to hack the things to pieces and even then he wasn't sure the zombie-like deformities wouldn't somehow continue fighting.

Mostyn studied the lay of the land. From the rise, the terrain dipped down and leveled off. About five hundred feet before the opening the land rose sharply ending in what looked like a flat area before the tunnel entrance.

"That five hundred foot sharp incline is going to be the problem," Mostyn informed H'tha-dub with his thoughts. "Especially with our former friends standing guard."

"How will we get passed the *y'm-bhi*, Mostyn Pierce?"

"I don't know, for sure. I do, however, have some ideas."

"What are these ideas?"

"Fire and swords."

"How will they help?"

"Swords, or axes, to dismember them, and fire to burn them up. Do you have some sort of flammable fuel?"

"I do not know, Mostyn Pierce."

"What powers the lamps?"

Into his mind came the word "electricity", and he nodded.

He sent his thoughts back to her. "Do you have any oil or fat?"

"I do not know, Mostyn Pierce. We can ask the slaves when we get back."

"Good. Let's go, then."

Mostyn took one last look at the gated opening and the mutilated forms of his former team members. Revenge. He wanted revenge, but knew that escape was his first priority.

16

MORNING. Or what passed for morning in K'n-yan. With the blue light never varying, the rhythm of the rest and active periods had been established by custom millennia ago. At least that is what H'tha-dub had told him, and Mostyn had no real reason to doubt her.

They'd woken to the smell of breakfast, the food set on the table by one of her slaves. As always, the food smelled good. This morning saw eggs, meat, the fungus that seemed to accompany every meal, some type of porridge, and fruit juice on the menu.

Yesterday, when they'd arrived back from their expedition, H'tha-dub had summoned the slaves and asked about oil and fat. She was told those items were regularly used in cooking and they came from the same abhumans that supplied the meat. Mostyn turned a little green at hearing that, thinking of the food he'd eaten that might have been cooked in oil derived from a corpse of something that might've been his cousin.

However, a different slave informed her that for the wagons and other things that needed lubrication, oil was obtained from a pool only a short distance from the city.

Mostyn asked to see some of the oil and H'tha-dub dispatched the slave to bring them a container of it. In short order, the slave returned with a bowl of dark liquid. Mostyn smelled the substance, touched a finger to it and rubbed the finger against his thumb to feel it, and then touched his finger to his tongue to taste the fluid.

When finished, he looked at H'tha-dub, and in Spanish, said, "This is crude oil. I can use it. I'll need more. A lot more." And he indicated the approximate size of the container he wanted filled with oil.

H'tha-dub relayed the information to the slave and sent him off to get the oil.

"I'll also need sticks of either green wood or something unburnable. About this long." He held his hands four feet apart.

"How many of these sticks will you need, Mostyn Pierce?"

"A dozen of them. And cloth. I'll need lots of cloth."

H'tha-dub sent slaves off to collect the materials. With the slaves off on their errands, she turned to Mostyn. "What are you going to make?"

"Torches, for light and to fight off the *y'm-bhi*."

H'tha-dub's eyes widened and she clapped her hands. "Oh, Mostyn Pierce, you are so very clever."

"I'll only be clever if I get us out of here."

The slaves brought back green wood, metal rods, and

the oil. Mostyn decided to use the metal rods. Mostly because they made a better club, in addition to not burning. He sat at the dining room table and tore the cloth into four-foot long strips, each strip about a foot wide. The next step was to wrap the cloth around one end of the rod to form a knob.

He held the finished product at arm's length before him and admired his handiwork. "Every bit as good as anything made by Indiana Jones."

"Who is this 'Indiana Jones'?" H'tha-dub asked.

Mostyn laughed. "A movie character. He would have loved being here."

"What is a 'movie'?"

Mostyn thought a moment before answering. "It's something like a play, except it is preserved on something called film to be watched by people in an amphitheater."

"What is 'film', Mostyn Pierce?"

"Good question. I'll explain some other time. Now I want to see if this thing works." He wiggled the torch and plunged the cloth end into the container of oil. "While that's soaking, I need you to find out where Candy and DC are. We can't leave without them."

"I will send a couple slaves to find out, if they can. It is best if I'm not seen as being too interested in your people."

Mostyn thought a moment, and then nodded.

H'tha-dub touched his cheek. "Your face tells me you are concerned about them. Your people."

"Yes, I am. They're good people. They don't deserve this."

"The ones called 'Candy' and 'DC', they seem to be enjoying themselves. At least that is what I've heard."

"I've spoken with Candy. She wants to stay. DC? I don't know. Maybe he does, too."

He took a look at the torch, checking the cloth to see if it had absorbed enough of the oil. "I think it's time to try this baby." Remembering he had no matches, he said, "I'll need some fire, or burning coals."

H'tha-dub summoned the slave who cooked for her and told him what she wanted. The slave departed and in a few minutes returned with a burning piece of wood and a red-hot coal.

Mostyn tried the coal first. Touching the petroleum soaked cloth to it, in less than thirty seconds the fuel ignited and Mostyn had his torch.

H'tha-dub clapped her hands. "Oh, Mostyn Pierce, that is amazing! What a new experience!"

"If you think this is something, there's a lot in my world that makes this nothing more amazing than a good night's sleep."

"I think I am going to like your world, Mostyn Pierce. So many new experiences!"

"Yeah, well, I need to put this somewhere so I can time how long it burns."

H'tha-dub summoned a slave and ordered her to hold the torch. Mostyn noticed fear in the slaves eyes and sent his thoughts to reassure her. "You'll be okay as long as you don't touch the flame."

While the torch was burning, Mostyn showed H'tha-dub how to make a torch and together they made the other eleven. Shortly after they finished their task, the torch the slave was holding flickered out. Mostyn guessed they'd most likely have a solid half-hour for each torch. They'd also need to carry with them something to light the first torch. A wet leather pouch holding a burning coal or two would do the trick. He'd read somewhere that was how ancient people transported fire before matches were invented. Flint and steel or friction methods being too slow and not overly reliable. Although tinderboxes had become pretty reliable by the time the first matches were invented. But Mostyn didn't think he had time to try to make a tinderbox.

All that was yesterday. Over their breakfast this morning, Mostyn sought to get more information from H'tha-dub.

He asked, "How far is the temple where my team's equipment is stored?"

"Not far. Less then the journey to the gate."

Mostyn walked to one of the windows. He looked out at the city of Tsath. Nothing here revealed the cruelty and barbarity of the K'n-yanian civilization. All looked peaceful and orderly. And if one didn't rock the boat, life here was nothing but one big party.

Slaves did the work and the freemen... Mostyn didn't know what the freemen did, probably some kind of work. Certainly they made up a share of the military. But as for the K'n-yanians themselves, the master class, they did nothing. They lived a hedonistic lifestyle gratifying every whim. And yet they were bored. Ennui was pervasive. They had everything and life was perfect. This was indeed utopia. What the philosophers of his world had dreamed of achieving, and yet the K'n-yanians were killing themselves out of boredom.

H'tha-dub came to his side. "You are longing for escape," she said in Spanish.

"Yes I am. What do the freemen do?"

"What do you mean?"

"Do they work?"

H'tha-dub laughed. "Oh, no, Mostyn Pierce. No one works. There are a few administrative duties carried out by the Council of Executives and *gn'agn*, otherwise no one works. That's what slaves are for."

"What about the military? You said some of the military was made up of freemen."

"Yes, the freemen are the officers and are our elite warriors. However, we have not fought a war for centuries and the use of the soldiers to capture you and your people is something we haven't had to do for many centuries, as well. So, as you can see, Mostyn Pierce, even the freemen who have duties very rarely ever need to perform them."

Mostyn's brow furrowed in thought. After a moment, he spoke. "So practically speaking, there's no difference between you and the freemen."

"That is correct. There is no practical difference between us. Even the rule not to mingle is rarely enforced. When it is, it is done so usually on a whim and even then not very often."

"I see." Mostyn felt a little downcast at the clarification she'd provided of the difference's between the two classes. If everyone was equal, then there was no chance of fomenting a class war. Escape from a well-ordered society was difficult. Escape from one in chaos was easier.

"We need to go to the temple and from the temple to the tunnel. I need to get a feel for how long it will take for us to get to the tunnel once we leave the city."

"We will be using *gyaa-yothn*?"

"Yes. We'll need them for speed and to carry the equipment."

"How many will you need?"

"One for everyone to ride and two extra for the equipment. Ten total."

"I have enough, Mostyn Pierce."

Breakfast finished, they moved to the sofa and before they were seated heard a knock on the door.

"Maybe it's our affection group!" H'tha-dub's face lit up and all Mostyn could think of was a teenager looking forward to a Friday night party. "You are welcome to enter!" she called out.

Materializing before them wasn't the affection group. It was none other than Ger-Hy'la-T'la.

"What the hell do you want?" Mostyn said in English.

In Mostyn's mind came the message, "You are summoned. We have captured one of your people, the one known as 'Jones'. He was attempting to force the one who calls herself 'Candy' to escape with him. Jones is to appear before the *gn'agn* shortly and they have summoned you."

Mostyn shook his head. Of all the harebrained stunts. Jones trying to rescue Slezak.

"What's going to happen to him?" Mostyn asked in Spanish.

Ger-Hy'la-T'la replied by sending his thoughts, "The *gn'agn* will decide. However, since he'd tried to escape with the one who does not wish to leave, he will probably be condemned to the amphitheater."

Mostyn shook his head and muttered in English, "Utopia. You're goddamn right it is."

17

BEFORE THE GN'AGN STOOD MOSTYN, DC Jones, Candy Slezak, and Ger-Hy'la-T'la. The conversation was conducted telepathically.

One of the tribunal 'spoke', "You who are called 'DC Jones' are accused of attempting to flee K'n-yan and, in the process of doing so, attempted to force the one known as 'Candy Slezak' to flee with you. What do you have to say for yourself?"

Jones replied out loud in English, and Mostyn translated telepathically, "I was not trying to leave. I merely wanted to talk with Candy. I saw her with her companion and wanted to speak with her."

"Is this true, Candy Slezak?"

Slezak looked past Ger-Hy'la-T'la to Jones and Mostyn. She licked her lips and then 'spoke', "Uh, um, I'm not sure what happened. I was pretty wasted."

"What is 'wasted'?" one of the tribunal asked.

"I, um, I was under the influence of zn'baa. All I know is

DC wanted to talk to me and my escort and his escort were trying to keep us apart and I really don't know what was going on."

A tribune gave a hand signal and two K'n-yanians entered the chamber, a young-looking man who was introduced as Gll'-yaa-Thaa, and a young-looking woman who was introduced as B'ya-lub.

The tribune in the center of the row asked, "Gll'-yaa-Thaa, did the upper worlder say he wanted to leave K'n-yan with the one known as 'Candy'?"

The man looked at Candy and then addressed the tribunal. "Yes. I was walking with Candy, when the upper worlder ran at us, pushed me aside, and took hold of Candy. I heard him say the word 'escape'."

The tribune looked at B'ya-lub. "Do you confirm the narrative of Gll'-yaa-Thaa?"

"I do not, Honorable One. The one known as 'DC Jones' said, 'There's Candy. I need to talk to her.' He then ran over to her. I ran after him and, because of the orders of the Council of Executives, I tried to separate the upper worlders, as did Gll'-yaa-Thaa. We were unable to do so until slaves were summoned and they overpowered DC Jones."

"Did he utter the word 'escape'?"

"Not to my knowledge, Honorable One."

Mostyn said out loud in Spanish, "In what language did DC Jones supposedly say the word 'escape'?"

Ger-Hy'la-T'la translated.

Gll'-yaa-Thaa answered, "K'n-yanian."

Mostyn smiled. The K'n-yanian had fallen into his trap.

He turned to Jones and asked in English, "Do you know any K'n-yanian?"

Jones chuckled. "Nothing for polite company."

"So I can imagine," Mostyn replied. In Spanish, he said, "DC Jones does not know K'n-yanian except for a few words that are not polite. He could not have spoken the word 'escape' in K'n-yanian."

Again Ger-Hy'la-T'la translated.

Gll'-yaa-Thaa protested. "He *thought* the word. It was clearly in my mind."

Mostyn sent out his thoughts, willing that everyone receive them. "Now he changes his story. Jones would have had to will his thoughts to Gll'-yaa-Thaa and, under the circumstances, I don't think that would've been possible, because Jones was focused on Candy Slezak. Gll'-yaa-Thaa is saying this because he wants Candy to stay and DC Jones poses a threat to that, as do all of us surface dwellers." *Might as well get the real issue out in the open,* he thought to himself.

Before Mostyn could confirm his assertion with Jones, B'ya-lub 'spoke'. "DC Jones is not very good at sending his thoughts in normal situations. In such excitement, I don't think he could have willed his thoughts to anyone. He is also not very good at learning our language. He has been teaching his affection group his language, called English. I do not think what Gll'-yaa-Thaa claims is possible for DC Jones to do."

The head tribune announced the *gn'agn* would confer and return with a decision. They stood and departed, proceeding to the back of the chamber and going through a door that was there.

Jones whispered to Mostyn, "Do you know Oppish?"

"What?"

"The code language. Like Pig Latin only you add 'op' after the consonants."

"No. Where did you learn it?"

"My nephew. I'll go slow. I thopinopkop Slopezopakop isop gopnope."

Mostyn sorted out the words and came up with, *I think Slezak is gone.* "Go on," he said.

"Fopounopdop thope topunnopelop."

Mostyn said under his breath, "Found the tunnel." To Jones, he said, "Go on."

"Bopya lopubop wopanoptopsop topo copomope wopithop usop."

Just what we need, Mostyn thought to himself. "Nopo."

Jones whispered, "Too late. Promised."

"Goddamn it, Jones. All right." Mostyn had no idea how they were going to take both B'ya-lub and H'tha-dub with them to the surface. Nevertheless, Jones's promise might prove useful.

The door at the end of the chamber opened and out filed the *gn'agn*. They took their seats and the head tribune sent his thoughts out to all present.

"No action will be taken against the one called 'DC Jones' because the narratives conflict. To avoid this happening in the future, Ger-Hy'la-T'la will establish a schedule so that no more than two upper worlders are outside their apartments at a time and they must be on opposite sides of the city from each other to ensure they will not meet. This is the decision of the *gn'agn*."

Slezak and Gll'-yaa-Thaa left first. Then Ger-Hy'la-T'la and Mostyn, followed by Jones and B'ya-lub. In the entry-way, Mostyn and Jones waited until Slezak and her watcher were out of sight. Then Jones and his watcher left. When they could no longer be seen, Ger-Hy'la-T'la escorted Mostyn back to H'tha-dub's apartment.

The K'n-yanian knocked on the door. "Jones was fortunate today," he informed Mostyn. "Next time, he will most likely be sent to the amphitheater to eliminate future disturbances."

H'tha-dub opened the door.

"Over my dead body," Mostyn replied in Spanish.

"That can be arranged," the K'n-yanian thought back. "Peace to you." And he departed.

18

MOSTYN WAS FURIOUS.

"Things did not go well for your DC Jones?" H'tha-dub was sitting on the sofa. Mostyn was pacing the floor in front of her.

"Oh, it all went just peachy."

"Why, then, are you angry, Mostyn Pierce?"

He sat and told her about the proceedings and emphasized the movement restriction and B'ya-lub. When he was finished, H'tha-dub, her eyes focused on nothing in particular, had a thoughtful look on her face.

After a few moments, Mostyn said, "Well?"

"I do not know B'ya-lub well. My impression of her, however, is not good, Mostyn Pierce. I will try to speak with her and assess the truth of her words."

"Do that. The sooner, the better. As for our little trip tomorrow…"

"You do not know when we can leave the apartment?"

"No. My understanding of how Ger-Hy'la-T'la operates,

he'll probably set up a fairly restrictive schedule. This isn't good. This isn't good at all."

"I will go now and talk with B'ya-lub."

"Be careful. If she is a spy, you don't want to let her know what we're planning."

"You have no need to be concerned, Mostyn Pierce. I have no desire to end my days in the amphitheater."

She kissed him and dematerialized.

Mostyn went to the drawer where he'd put the notes of the information he'd come across in the library. He stretched out on the couch and reviewed them.

Suddenly, he had a thought. *If we're restricted above ground, what's to prevent us moving below ground?*

He sat up and said out loud, "There has to be some kind of sewer system to carry away the wastewater. And if there is a sewer system, there has to be access to it in order to carry out repairs, check on problems, do inspections, and the like. If I can find a map of the sewer system, that could provide us with the best way to gather everyone together and at least get out of the city undetected."

Mostyn stood and began pacing. He continued talking out loud. "Throughout history invaders have gained access to cities through sewers, or a river passing through the city, or work tunnels. People have escaped from cities the same way. A map of the sewer system and the nearest access point and we're in business."

He also realized that with the new restrictions in place, he was more dependent than ever on H'tha-dub. She was a beautiful woman. In some ways, very naïve and innocent. Mostyn smiled. "Don't kid yourself," he said out loud, as he continued pacing. "She isn't a child. She's over nine hundred years old. She's seen and no doubt done things that would make your hair curl, pal."

No, H'tha-dub was no innocent. What he was convinced of was that for some reason he couldn't fully fathom, she'd fallen in love with him.

"All I can say is, she must've really fallen for Zamacona and then transferred all of that feeling to me," Mostyn mused out loud. "Kind of like She and Kallikrates and Leo Vincey." He paused, and then added, "And I fear I'm just as cursed as those two lovers."

The air shimmered, and immediately H'tha-dub appeared.

She sighed. "My love. You cannot possibly know the sorrow I feel being apart from you." She came to Mostyn, who'd stopped his pacing, put her arms around him, kissed his lips, and laid her head upon his shoulder.

If not for Dotty, Mostyn thought, *I could love this woman.*

H'tha-dub pulled away, kissed him, and sat on the sofa. "I did manage to find B'ya-lub, and in doing so found the apartment for DC Jones."

"That's good! What did you find out?"

"They were copulating."

"Oh."

"I will continue to try to talk to her."

"I'm not sure we can afford the time." Mostyn sat next to her. "Am I correct in assuming there is a sewer system underneath Tsath?"

"I have never thought about this, but the water for the

city must come from somewhere and the used water must then go somewhere. Does it not?"

"It does indeed. Is there access to the system? In my world, there are holes in the ground covered by round, heavy metal plates. Do you have anything like that here?"

"I do not know, Mostyn Pierce."

"How do people access the system for repairs?"

"I do not know. That is something slaves would do."

Frustration showed on Mostyn's face. "We need to get back to the library. I have to find a map of the sewer system under Tsath."

"How do we do that, Mostyn Pierce?"

"Can you dematerialize both of us?"

"You are so devious, Mostyn Pierce! Another new experience! A lover who is devious and conniving. Oh, Mostyn Pierce..."

"Focus. Please."

She sighed.

He repeated his question and she thought a moment before answering. "I have never dematerialized a person before. I could try."

"But you have dematerialized other things?"

"Yes. On occasion."

"So it's possible you could dematerialize both of us?"

"Yes."

There was a tremor in the floor and a dull boom reached their ears.

Mostyn jumped up. "Bardon! He must be launching a major attack."

"What is 'Bardon', Mostyn Pierce?"

"My boss. A round little Englishman who knows more about the arcane and forbidden knowledge than does half the solar system."

"Is this good?"

There was another tremor and dull boom.

"Oh, it's very good. It means the cavalry is on its way."

"What is this 'cavalry'?"

"I'll explain later." Mostyn went to the window. A perfect view of the street. There were people about. Most seemed unconcerned about the tremors and booms.

"What do we do, Mostyn Pierce?"

He went to the drawer and took out the map of the city he'd "borrowed" from the library. Suddenly, there was panic on the street. He went to the window. People were screaming, pointing upwards, and running. Mostyn dropped the map, ran to the door, threw it open, ran down the short length of the hallway, out the main door, and into the street. H'tha-dub was right behind him.

Mostyn looked up and said, "Well, I'll be damned."

There, flying through the air, were drones. Scores of them. Mostyn waved his arms and several drones stopped, apparently focused on him, and then continued on their way.

"Bardon now knows at least I'm here."

"This is good?"

"Very. The drones will transmit where they saw me, and any of the others on my team, and that's where the rescue attempt will be focused."

"Your people are coming to get you?"

"You bet they are, honey!"

Mostyn and H'tha-dub watched the drones, while the street filled with slaves and *y'm-bhi*. One *y'm-bhi* with six arms and four legs had two crossbows. He'd shoot one, while reloading the other. In the span of a minute, he knocked down five drones. Another slave, using a kind of slingshot on a rifle stock, was equally deadly in knocking down drones.

The drones clustered together and began firing on the K'n-yanian defense force. Several slaves fell. The *y'm-bhi* were unaffected and kept firing away at the drones, with several more falling to the ground.

Another squad of slaves rushed to the battle and fired a couple dozen projectiles at the drones. To Mostyn's amazement the projectiles joined together forming a single large projectile that ripped through the cluster of drones, taking out at least half.

H'tha-dub uttered, *"Tulu-t'agn!"*, and bowed.

Mostyn thought back to his reading of the Binger files. "The Tulu metal!" he said out loud. "How clever. The projectiles, made of the metal, are attracted to each other, and many small units become one deadly large one."

He was surprised the K'n-yanians had resorted to using the metal, because, according to what Howard Langley had reported from Zamacona's document, the K'n-yanians revered the metal. The stuff supposedly having come to earth from wherever the great Cthulhu himself had originated.

The drones had dispersed and were flying back in the direction of the tunnel opening.

"Looks like the party's over," Mostyn said, in Spanish. "I suppose we'd best get back inside."

"Yes, Mostyn Pierce. We would not want one of the counsel, or the *gn'agn*, or one of their agents, to see you."

They returned to the apartment and Mostyn, picking up a map, went to the dining room table, where he spread it out.

"Are you able to show me on this map, where my team members are located?"

H'tha-dub joined him and studied the layout of the city.

"Yes, I can show you." She pointed, "Here is DC Jones."

"Can you mark the map?"

Her eyes lit up. "Oh, yes, Mostyn Pierce!"

She fairly ran from the room and returned with a pen and a bottle of the K'n-yanian green ink.

She unstoppered the bottle and dipped the pen into the liquid. "This is so exciting, Mostyn Pierce! I haven't used this pen for two hundred years! How do I mark the map?"

"Just make an 'x'."

"How do I make this 'x'?"

"Like this." He crossed two lines to show her. "Put one where each of my team members are."

She did so, and there was a big smile on her face. "What is next, Mostyn Pierce?"

"We need to mark who is at each 'x'."

"I write the person's name?"

"Yes."

"I do not know how to do that."

"How about this, I write the names in my language to show you?"

She pouted. "But I want to write."

"Here, then. I'll guide your hand." He moved next to her and took her hand in his.

"Ooh, Mostyn Pierce, this is *so very* exciting!" She nuzzled his ear.

"Focus, my pet, or we'll never get to my world."

She nipped his earlobe. "Oh, all right."

Mostyn guided H'tha-dub's hand and wrote the name of each one of his team members name by an 'x'. When finished, he looked over the map. The only one missing was Slezak.

"Where the hell does Slezak live?"

"She seems to always be with her affection group, moving from apartment to apartment, and going to temple."

"Damn. We're going to have to find her when we're ready to leave. Probably, we'll have to kidnap her."

"What is this 'kidnap'?"

"Take her against her will."

"Is that wise, Mostyn Pierce?"

"Probably not."

"Then we should not do this kidnap."

"You're probably right. Let me think about it. For now, our next stop is the library. I need a map of the sewer system."

"Very well, Mostyn Pierce. Now? Do we leave now?"

"Now is as good a time as any."

H'tha-dub wrapped her arms around Mostyn and after a moment, the two disappeared.

19

MOSTYN AND H'THA-DUB spent most of the "afternoon" in the library. Because the place was rarely used, there was no staff on site and the two had to fend for themselves in trying to locate information regarding the building and maintenance of the great city of Tsath. In their previous visit, Mostyn had learned the K'n-yanian cataloging system. This time, the issue was how the information they were looking for was classified.

After numerous attempts, they finally found the section on the history of the city and another on civil planning. It was in the latter section they found the maps. They took them back to H'tha-dub's apartment, after she dematerialized Mostyn, the paper, and herself.

Mostyn found being dematerialized quite disconcerting. The feeling reminded him of accounts he'd read of out-of-body experiences told by those who had survived clinical death and those persons who had unintentionally or intentionally left their bodies. Except he had no physical body to look at, because it was nothing more then a cloud of atoms.

Somehow he saw what was around him, not having eyes, and somehow he sped along the streets, went through the walls of buildings, not having any legs. The weightlessness and the feeling of not being in himself filled him with anxiety. In addition, the speed at which they traveled made him feel nauseous. For that, however, he had only himself to blame, as he had told H'tha-dub to hurry.

He could "see" her and she, him. They could talk to each other; that is, they could send their thoughts to each other. And he felt the texture and weight of the maps he held. For lack of a better way to describe the feeling, Mostyn thought he felt like a ghost.

Rematerialized in H'tha-dub's apartment, Mostyn was very glad for his body to be back "together". He walked over to the table and compared the map of the city with a map of the sewer system. They weren't identical. The sewer system map was apparently the older of the two, at least that was Mostyn's guess. Because H'tha-dub confirmed the existence of areas of the city that didn't appear on the sewer map.

With the two maps lined up, Mostyn studied the sewer layout in order to identify the most direct route that would take them from the city to the temple where their equipment was stored.

A slave entered with food and Mostyn reluctantly set the maps aside.

"The time has come to eat, Mostyn Pierce. I am famished, for you deprived me of my dinner."

"You poor thing."

"I am not poor."

"Just an expression."

"Oh." She then smiled at him.

They sat and began eating.

"Have you worked everything out, Mostyn Pierce?"

"As much as I can. While you are collecting everyone, a slave will take the *gyaa-yothn* to the temple. Once everyone is at the start point, we'll go through the sewers, there is an entrance a block away, and an exit near the road that goes passed the temple. We'll get the equipment and make for the tunnel as fast as we can.

"Once we've reached the tunnel, we'll fight our way through the guards if we have to and hopefully make our escape."

"The plan sounds so simple."

"It is. So probably a thousand things will pop up to derail it."

"Maybe not, Mostyn Pierce."

"Maybe not, but likely yes."

"If we are caught…"

"I know. We don't want to be caught."

"No, we do not."

In Mostyn's mind flashed the images of his deformed team members.

———

Mostyn did his best. In the end, he couldn't avoid her. He needed her. Not in the sexual sense. He needed her cooperation, and to secure that he had to give in to her insistence that they be husband and wife.

He lay in the bed on his back. Even though not in the mood, he had to admit the sex was exquisite. She lay next to him and drew circles on his chest with her finger.

"Do I please you, Mostyn Pierce?"

Dotty flashed through his mind and he pushed the image away.

"Yes, H'tha-dub, you please me. Any man would be lucky to have you for his wife." That last sentence was absolutely true. Mostyn had no doubt she could make any man feel like a king.

She snuggled closer to him. He turned and kissed the tip of her nose.

"Let us copulate again." Her voice was heavy with desire.

"Can't. We need to leave during the rest period."

She bolted upright. "Today?"

"The rest period is about to start any time now, isn't it?"

"It is."

"Good. We can't wait. I don't want your people to seal the tunnel to prevent my people from coming through, which would mean we can't get out."

"Oh, Mostyn Pierce, I am tired of this. Why can you not stay here?"

"For the same reason Zamacona couldn't. It's not in our nature. We top-worlders don't like to be caged up."

"Very well." Her glum expression suddenly brightened. "Let us bathe together before we depart."

"Okay. But we can't linger. We have a lot to do."

H'tha-dub drew the water while Mostyn took another look at the maps. He committed as much to memory as he could, and then joined H'tha-dub in the bathroom.

Bath completed, H'tha-dub sent two slaves to the temple with the *gyaa-yothn*. Mostyn made sure they took the torches, oil, and several coals from the fire.

The next stage of his plan was perhaps the most risky. To each teammate's apartment, H'tha-dub had to travel in a dematerialized state. Once inside their apartment, she'd rematerialize, seize the person, dematerialize both of them, and bring the person back with her to her apartment where Mostyn was waiting.

Mostyn cautioned her that if she could not abduct the team member without being seen, she was to go on to the next one. The questionable ones she'd go back for after the others had been secured.

First on the list was Jones. Mostyn wanted his trained agent first in order to fill him in on the plan. But when H'tha-dub returned, Mostyn saw Zink and not Jones.

"He was copulating, Mostyn Pierce."

Mostyn muttered, "Goddamn Jones", and sent her off to bring back the next one on the list.

Beames arrived, and she was followed by Jones. H'tha-dub managed to take him while he was in the bathroom.

"Glad you could make the party, Jones. Now all we need is to get you some clothes."

"We're leaving?"

"No. This is a Christmas party."

Beames and Zink didn't succeed in stifling their laughter.

"B'ya-lub wants to come with us," Jones protested.

"Can't. Too much risk."

"But she's been very helpful. She found out where Slezak spends most of her time."

"Where? Show me on this map."

Jones studied the layout and then put his finger on the paper. "There. She's probably there."

H'tha-dub returned with Baker, and Mostyn motioned for her to come to him.

"Jones needs clothes and here is where we think Candy Slezak is. Bring her next. No matter what."

"Is that wise, Mostyn Pierce?"

"No. But I want her here so we all have time to talk some sense into her."

"Very well." H'tha-dub gave an order to a slave and then was gone.

"We're making a run for it tonight?" Willie Lee Baker asked.

"That's the plan, Willie Lee. Things aren't getting any better for us as the days go by."

The slave returned with clothes and gave them to Jones. She left and he put them on.

Zink said, "This supposed utopia they have here, it's the worst dystopian nightmare anyone can imagine. I was forced to watch my affection group torture a slave for their entertainment — while we were eating! God, the Romans at their worst were more civilized."

Beames's voice was soft, but the emotion was hard. "In my group, one day, they brought in a slave. The men raped her while the women mutilated her. I tried not to watch, but they made me. I don't remember how many times I threw up."

Mostyn put his arm around Beames and gave her a squeeze. "With a little luck, this will soon be over."

A tremor gently shook the room and a dull boom reached their ears.

"Sounds like Bardon's back at it," Jones said.

"That it does," Mostyn replied.

"Are we going after our equipment first?" Jones asked.

"Yes."

"B'ya-lub told me where the equipment was being stored," Jones continued.

"She did?"

"Yep. Been out there to the temple and saw it for myself." Jones was beaming.

Mostyn sat. "This isn't good."

Jones had a puzzled expression on his face. "What do you mean 'this isn't good'?"

"H'tha-dub has a reason to believe B'ya-lub may be a spy."

"No! I don't believe it, Mostyn. She said she loves me and wants to leave with us."

"I suppose every female spy has said something similar from the beginning of time. Why? Because we men almost always fall for such shit. Think with your big head, Jones."

"No. I can't…"

H'tha-dub reappeared with a screaming Candy Slezak.

"She was very difficult, Mostyn Pierce."

"How'd you get her to come?" Mostyn asked.

"I told her I would leave her in a dematerialized state if she did not come with me."

Mostyn chuckled. "Gag her. We can't have all that racket."

H'tha-dub summoned a slave and when she appeared, gave her orders. Moments later the slave was back with cloth and a rope.

Jones and Zink bound and gagged Slezak.

"Mostyn Pierce, something is happening by the tunnel. There are loud noises and there is an odd greenish glow coming from there."

"None of this is sounding good," Mostyn replied. "B'ya-lub knows where our equipment is stored."

A noise outside drew their attention.

"Everyone down!" Mostyn ordered, while he motioned for H'tha-dub to come with him outside.

On the street, they saw drones in the sky. They were firing some sort of laser weapon. This time, however, Mostyn watched the K'n-yanians mount a different defense. In a matter of moments, the cluster of drones disappeared.

"What the hell?" Mostyn muttered.

"They dematerialized them," H'tha-dub said.

Mostyn nodded. "Of course. Why didn't they do that on the first attack?"

"Because the *y'm-bhi* and slaves do not have that ability."

"So the K'n-yanians themselves are now conducting the defense."

"Yes, Mostyn Pierce."

"Things must be getting serious. Get Kemper. We have to leave as soon as possible."

H'tha-dub touched Mostyn's cheek and kissed him. "I do all of this to be with you, Mostyn Pierce." And she vanished.

Mostyn returned to the apartment and told the group what he saw.

"This can't be good," Beames said.

Zink agreed, "No, Esther, it isn't. None of this is good."

Mostyn went to Slezak. "Candy, I'm going to pull down the gag. If you scream, it goes back. Understand?"

She nodded her head.

Mostyn pulled the gag down. "Candy, this place is not for us. You have family. Friends."

"I want to stay, Pierce. I like it here."

Beames said, "Do you like the torture?"

"Yeah, I kinda do." A cocky little lilt was in Slezak's voice.

"You're sick," Beames replied, and walked away.

"I like these people, Pierce. I'll fight you if you try to take me with you."

"Candy, you are an outworlder. These people are xeno-phobic. They will never trust you."

"They trust me just fine, Pierce. They take me every-where in the city and out to the countryside. They show me everything and I tell them all about our world. Yeah, they're into mutilation and torture. But are they any different from us, Mostyn? We have BDSM, cock fights, and dogfights. We have boxing and roller derby and foot-ball. We have rape and murder and sexual abuse, for God's sake. And look at how we treat the animals we eat. It's horrible! Are these people truly any different then we are?"

"But we're moving away from that stuff," Mostyn said, "we're trying to be better."

"Yeah, right. Well, these people *are* better. They have one fault. Otherwise, this society is perfect. It's fucking utopia, Pierce. Everyone truly is equal."

"What about the slaves?" Zink asked.

"Most of them are dead," Slezak shot back. "How are they any different than a machine?"

Jones sat next to her. "Look, Candy—"

"Go fuck yourself, DC. I heard all about the big outworlder and his pet K'n-yanian."

"But—"

"Get the hell out of my face, DC. You're nothing but a typical man looking to get his rocks off. Screw you."

Jones moved away.

"Don't take me back, Pierce. I'm happy here and I want to stay."

Mostyn looked at the group. "Well?"

Beames shrugged. "Let her stay. Getting out of here is going to be hard enough as it is."

Zink nodded, and said, "I agree."

Mostyn look at Jones and said his name.

"Whatever she wants," he replied.

Mostyn looked at Baker. "What Jones said."

The room quivered and a boom sounded in the distance. There was a shimmer, and then H'tha-dub and Dotty Kemper appeared. When Kemper saw Mostyn, her face broke into a smile. She ran to him, threw her arms around him, and kissed him with abandon.

Surprise showed on H'tha-dub's face and then a black cloud descended. She pointed at Mostyn, yelled a string of K'n-yanian words, and disappeared.

Slezak burst out laughing, and she became everyone's focus. "Man, Pierce, I think you just fucked this up big time."

"What did she say?" he asked.

"She said, if I translate freely, you're a bigger dick then Pánfilo. You used her love to get what you wanted when all along you already had a wife."

Kemper pushed him away. "What? What's this wife shit?"

"Look, Dotty—"

"Don't you 'look, Dotty' me, Pierce Mostyn. You were fucking her, weren't you?"

"Dotty."

"Weren't you?" Dotty's voice was loud and harsh.

"I did it to save your ass!"

"You did it just to get a piece of ass when you couldn't have mine!"

Slezak was howling with laughter. Jones had a smug look on his face. Beames looked perturbed, and Zink was expressionless. Baker, sitting off by himself, shook his head.

"Look, the price for her cooperation was marriage," Mostyn explained.

"Marriage!" Kemper's voice shot up into the high register, and was practically squeaking.

"So I agreed. I saw no other way for us to get out of here. We needed someone on the inside."

Kemper wasn't buying it. "What you wanted on the inside was your dick. Goddamn you, Pierce. God. Damn. You!"

Tears ran down Kemper's cheeks and she swiped at them with the backs of her hands.

Mostyn was about to say something, thought better of it, and instead changed his entire demeanor. "Enough. What's done is done. We have to leave *now*. There is no telling what H'tha-dub or B'ya-lub will do. We can't dawdle."

He quickly explained the plan. "Any questions?"

Kemper asked, "Are we taking Slezak?"

"No," Mostyn replied. "She wants to stay." To the linguist, he said, "Are you going to betray us?"

"Don't have to," she replied. "You won't get far."

"We might not, but we have to try."

"Suit yourself. You going to leave me tied up?"

"No. Jones, untie her."

Jones complied. When he was done, she said, "Thanks, Jonesy." And gave him a peck on the cheek. "After they make you a *y'm-bhi*, I'm going to ask them to give you to me."

Jones gave her a hard look. "I really liked you. Glad I found out what a cunt you really are before anything got serious."

She spit in his face. Jones wiped it away and stood up.

"We're done here. Let's go," Mostyn ordered.

The ground shook and a boom sounded in the distance. Mostyn led his people out into the street.

———

20

MOSTYN HAD COUNTED on H'tha-dub using her dematerializing ability to get them into the sewer system. With her gone, and not knowing if she'd betrayed them, Mostyn decided to forego using the sewer and proceed directly overland. He didn't want to get trapped like the proverbial rats in a maze.

Off in the distance, there was a definite green glow coming from the direction of the tunnel. What that meant, Mostyn wasn't certain. But if he had to bet money on it, he'd wager something supernatural was in the air. The question was, which side was recruiting other-dimensional, or inter-dimensional help. Or maybe both sides were. If that was the case, then God help the planet.

Being the rest period, there weren't a lot of people on the streets. Lights shone from many of the upper floor windows of the tall buildings, and Mostyn guessed that some of the K'n-yanians were watching whatever was going on at the tunnel. Much like the picnickers who went out to watch the First Battle of Bull Run.

Only Jones had been to the old and abandoned temple of the hideously grotesque deity Tsathoggua, and the one who was arguably the most powerful and destructive of the K'n-yanian pantheon. According to Langley's recounting of Zamacona's narrative, that was the reason the monster was no longer worshiped. Mostyn let Jones lead the way.

The group briskly walked across the expanse of park land. Jones in the lead, followed by Doctors Beames, Zink, and Kemper, and finally Mostyn. Making faster time than if they'd gone through the sewer tunnels, they arrived at the temple to find the two docile slaves with the *gyaa-yothn*. No one else appeared to be around.

"Beames, Kemper, secure our transportation. Zink, Baker, take point." Mostyn indicated where he wanted them to watch. "Jones, you're with me."

Standing on either side of the door, Mostyn pushed it open. Out came a half-dozen *y'm-bhi* with spears. Jones wrenched the weapon away from one of the live-dead and shoved it through the thing's head. When that didn't stop it, Jones picked it up and threw it at several of the creatures. Yet on they came.

"Damn," Jones said, "that always works in the zombie movies."

Mostyn holding one in a full Nelson, called out, "They aren't zombies!" He broke the thing's neck and it still flailed about even when two of the other *y'm-bhi* jabbed their spears into its body trying to get at Mostyn.

"How are we going to kill these things?" Jones shouted,

using one like the blade on a bulldozer to force a path into the temple.

"Fire!" Mostyn yelled. "Beames, Kemper! Light the torches!"

"With what?" Kemper shouted. "Your infidelity?"

"There's a leather pouch with hot coals in it," Mostyn yelled back.

Zink and Baker joined in the melee to relieve Mostyn and Jones, but nothing they did would stop the already dead, yet alive creatures.

A *y'm-bhi* wrestled Zink to the ground. Another was menacing Baker with a spear, which he frantically kept batting away by using a broken spear shaft like a bat. Mostyn was down and frantically trying to stop one of the living-dead from throttling the life out of him. Jones, in the temple, had grabbed a knife and, with back against a wall, was trying to hold three of the creatures at bay in the dark.

Having gotten a couple torches lit, Beames and Kemper, flaming torches in hand, and carrying jars of oil, were dousing and igniting the *y'm-bhi*. The live-dead beings flared up like dry kindling and in a matter of moments collapsed in burning heaps.

"There, Mostyn. I saved your ass and didn't fuck anyone to do it."

"Dotty."

"Don't. You. Dare. Dotty. Me. Now, Mister Boss Man, get us the hell out of here."

They grabbed their equipment, loaded it onto the *gyaa-yothn,* and mounted the hideous beasts.

"Listen up, everyone," Mostyn began, "we ride for our lives. Follow me!"

Before Mostyn could spur his creature on, in front of him appeared H'tha-dub. Standing proud and erect, her head thrown back, she pointed at Mostyn. Her thoughts rang out so all could hear. "You betrayed my love. You used me, though you love another. I betrayed my people for you, and now I have no home. I die in the amphitheater or I leave with you. Since I do not wish to become a *y'm-bhi,* you must take me with you. You, Mostyn Pierce, owe me that much."

"Yes, I do. Mount up."

"I will lead," she informed them. "The freemen are on their way." H'tha-dub mounted a *gyaa-yothn* and urged it into a shambling gallop.

"Follow her!" Mostyn ordered. Behind him, he heard Kemper say, "Shit."

21

NOT FOLLOWING THE ROAD, H'tha-dub led Mostyn and his team across the countryside. The shambling monstrosities were not as fast as horses, but they moved faster than Mostyn and his people could on foot. And because of their rudimentary intelligence, they could be given instructions in a way a horse never could.

Quicker than Mostyn thought possible, they found themselves on the road that led to the tunnel. When they reached the crest of the hill and the tunnel entrance was visible in the distance, they rested the *gyaa-yothn*. Before them was a war zone. The tunnel entrance was three times larger than before and the stone was blackened as though by fire.

The field was littered with partially buried robots and booted feet sticking out of the ground. Scores, maybe hundreds, of drones lay smashed on the ground. The tunnel entrance shimmered green and the air near the domed roof also shimmered with a greenish hue.

To their left, some distance away, stood an army of what was probably thousands of *y'm-bhi* and slaves, and several dozen freeman and K'n-yanians mounted on *gyaa-yothn*.

"Good God," Baker muttered.

"So much for the technologically superior," Kemper said.

"We have company," Jones called out.

Mostyn turned and saw, in the distance, maybe twenty riders heading their way. He began issuing orders.

"Jones, get the machine gun ready. Baker, help him with the ammo feed."

The men dismounted and Baker said, "We're on it."

"The rest of you, look lively now. Dismount and get ready to fight should any of them break through.

Mostyn sent his thoughts to H'tha-dub asking her to tell the *gyaa-yothn* to lie down and form a living wall for everyone to take cover behind. She did so, and the docile creatures complied.

Up the rise the riders came. When they were about a hundred yards out, Jones opened fire, sending a furious stream of death into the enemy's ranks. And down they went. Two managed to veer off and avoid the carnage. Kemper took out one with a round from her rifle and H'tha-dub dematerialized the other. When he rematerialized, his feet were sticking out of the butt of a now dead *gyaa-yothn*.

Amazement was all over Kemper's face. "Now *that* is something *I* have to learn."

H'tha-dub smiled, and said in heavily accented English, "I teach."

The riders and their mounts lay dead and dying. However, the noise of the skirmish had attracted the attention of a unit of live-dead and they began marching towards Mostyn's group.

"Damn," Jones said. "It's those zombies that won't die."

"Get the torches and oil ready," Mostyn ordered.

The *y'm-bhi*, armed with swords, spears, and crossbows, charged up the rise. Burning torches and oil ready, Mostyn and his people met the charge. Zink took an arrow in the thigh. Beames doused a *y'm-bhi* with oil and set it on fire. It dropped its sword, ran into another live-dead, and they fell together in a burning heap.

Mostyn knocked down one of the live-dead and yanked a spear away from another, when it disappeared. He silently thanked H'tha-dub, and shoved the spear through the head of yet another of the zombi-like creatures, pinning it to the ground.

Jones and Baker, each with a sword, were hacking off heads and limbs. One headless and armless corpse was stumbling around until Beames set it on fire.

Using her torch as a club, Kemper bashed a *y'm-bhi* in the head and its hair caught fire. She doused it with oil and it turned into a human torch. Another zombie-like creature came at her and Kemper parried the thing's sword thrust. She then turned and smashed in its face with her torch. The creature staggered back, and the wounded Zink splashed it with oil and set it on fire. The thing took off running and impaled itself on another creature's spear. The two tumbled down the hill in a burning heap.

A rider suddenly appeared. Beames disappeared and only her hips and legs reappeared, sticking out of the ground. Kemper fired her revolver and the bullet struck the K'n-yanian in the chest. Mostyn fired his pistol. The forty-five caliber hollow point punched its way through the man's face and exited the back of his skull in a shower a bone, blood, and brains. He fell off his *gyaa-yothn*, his body twitching and jerking until it lay still.

H'tha-dub saved Beames from suffocating by dematerializing and then rematerializing her above ground. She then turned her attention to the few remaining *y'm-bhi* attackers and dematerialized them.

Around Jones and Baker were a slew of animated body parts jumping and rolling around. The most disconcerting were the hands crawling crab-like, trying to fulfill their mission. H'tha-dub dematerialize them.

"Look!" Zink exclaimed.

Everyone looked to where he was pointing. The green glow at the tunnel entrance was thick as heavy fog and iridescent.

"Look up there!" Baker yelled.

High in the atmosphere, another thick iridescent green cloud had formed.

"What the hell?" Jones muttered.

"That's exactly what's happening," Mostyn said.

Up in the air, a black line appeared in the green cloud and gradually grew wider. Tentacles appeared and pushed the opening even wider until it was a large black hole. A hole in the fabric of space and time.

"Oh my God," Kemper shouted.

Out of the hole crawled a noxiously blasphemous monstrosity of immense proportions. An amoeboid thing with bulging yellow eyes that floated on its formless body. Scores of tentacles protruded out of the thing. It hovered in the air and then slowly descended towards the ground.

"What the hell have the K'n-yanians done?" Mostyn asked, his voice laced with fear.

Out of the tunnel entrance poured a gelatinous blob, radiating a rainbow of iridescent colors across its undulating surface. When its formless bulk was free from the tunnel, like an enormous blimp, it launched itself into the air.

"Oh my God," Kemper said. "Bardon must be at it, too."

Everyone on the ground watched the two inter-dimensional obscenities collide and begin a titanic duel. Lightning flashed and thunder boomed.

Bardon's blob formed itself into a six-fingered hand and wrapped its fingers around the tentacled amoeboid creature. The amoeboid thing countered by wrapping tentacles around the blob. Each entity trying to wrap itself around the other as an amoeba around a particle of food.

Mouths appeared and disappeared. Lightning bursts flashed from each being. And round and round they spun like an inter-dimensional ouroboros.

"Now!" Mostyn yelled. "To the tunnel! Run!"

Across the wreckage-strewn plain they ran, while above them the colossal insanities battled in the sky.

Up the steep slope they climbed. On the edge, they saw six *y'm-bhi*.

"Grenades," Mostyn called out.

Jones nodded and passed them out to everyone.

"On my command," Mostyn said. "Pull pin. And throw!"

The grenades came raining down on the *y'm-bhi* and exploded, ripping the living dead into chunks of blasted flesh and bone.

"Now, into the tunnel. Jones, you first. The rest follow," Mostyn ordered.

The team members and H'tha-dub followed Jones into the tunnel that would take them to the upper world and freedom. Various body parts of the live-dead slaves were still animated, but did not pose a threat. Kemper kicked the shrapnel pitted head of one *y'm-bhi* like a soccer ball as it tried to bite her foot, and watched it bounce down the steep slope before she turned and disappeared into the tunnel.

Baker entered the tunnel, and that left Mostyn. He turned and looked at the dueling entities that were from somewhere not of this universe. Blasphemies that nature itself cannot comprehend. He watched Bardon's blob, at least he thought it the thing Bardon must've summoned, increase its size several times and wrap itself around the tentacled thing as a sheet of plastic wrap around a piece of meat. A brilliant light shown inside and then all was dark.

Bardon's creature, a colorless blimp-like thing, slowly settled to the ground. All Mostyn could imagine is that perhaps it was wounded. Once it had settled on the ground, he watched it flatten out and then slowly the iridescent rainbow began to ripple across its surface. Then it was gone! And charging across the plain were thousands of *y'm-bhi* and slaves.

"Holy shit!" Mostyn exclaimed. "They must've dematerialized it!"

He turned and ran into the tunnel. A hundred feet in, he met Baker.

"The others are on their way out," he said. "I waited for you."

"They're coming," Mostyn panted. "By the thousands. Let's go!"

The two men ran after their compatriots and soon caught up to them due to the wounded Zink.

"Keep going!" Mostyn yelled. "They're coming. Thousands! Give me the grenades." The others gave him the four remaining grenades.

On they pushed, up the incline, Mostyn remaining at the back of the group, and when Zink couldn't go on, Jones hoisted him up in a fireman's carry.

"Promise me you'll go on a diet when we get back," Jones grunted.

"Promise," Zink replied.

Behind them they could hear the dull patter of feet. The enemy was in pursuit.

Beames stumbled, and Kemper caught her before she fell.

"God, I don't think I can make it," the ethnologist panted.

"Think of Patty or Eliza. You don't want that."

"No. I don't." From somewhere inside her, came additional resolve and she and Kemper ran on, following the others. At last the group burst into the chamber where they'd fought the K'n-yanians and been captured.

"Go on," Mostyn yelled to the others. He swept the chamber with his helmet-mounted flashlight. And that's when he spotted the computer assembly sitting on top of a box where the pedestal and statue of Cthulhu had been. He looked across to the opposite alcove and saw that the statue of Shub-Niggurath was no longer there, either, and in its place was another computer.

"God bless you, Doctor Bardon," Mostyn murmured, and followed his people up the tunnel.

He caught up with Jones, who, for all his hulking strength, was obviously tired. They were met by H'tha-dub, who'd dropped back from the others.

"I will take this man." She pointed to Zink.

"Thank you, H'tha-dub," Mostyn said.

She and Zink disappeared.

Jones looked at Mostyn. "So you were really doing her?"

"Shut up, Jones."

The junior agent burst out laughing. "Well, I'll be damned. Mister Up-Tight—"

"Enough. Let's go. They're coming, and Bardon has a surprise for them. One we don't want to be around to share."

They ran as fast as their legs could carry them. They'd managed to put some eight hundred feet between them and the chamber, when the blast occurred. The concussive force knocked them down and pelted them with dust and stones.

"Shit," Jones groaned. "Wish to hell he would have warned us."

"On that, I agree," Mostyn replied, and slowly sat up. "God, my ears."

"Yeah," Jones agreed. "A frickin' bell choir's in my head."

They stood and continued trotting up the passage. At the bottom of the stairway, they met Kemper, Beames, and Baker.

"Where's your *wife* and Zink?" Kemper asked.

"She's not my wife, and she took Zink on ahead," Mostyn replied.

"I hope she teaches me how to do that," Kemper said.

"Beam me up, Scotty." Jones chuckled, and he and Kemper bumped fists.

"Bardon blew the tunnel; we shouldn't have anymore problems."

Slowly, they climbed the stairs. About halfway up, they met H'tha-dub and Zink. Beames was the first to notice.

"Where's the arrow?" she asked, pointing at Zink's leg.

In Spanish, H'tha-dub said, "I dematerialized it and then rematerialized his flesh together."

"Oh, my God," Beames said in English, and then explained what the K'n-yanian had done.

Kemper's eyes were big and round. "She just obsoleted surgery."

Behind them, the air shimmered. Mostyn yelled, "Enemy!" And eight beings materialized, two K'n-yanians, and six *y'm-bhi* — the mutilated forms of their former comrades.

Jones, Mostyn, and Kemper fired their weapons and the two K'n-yanians perished in a hail of lead. Then the *y'm-bhi* were upon them.

The torches having gone out some time ago, it was now brutal hand-to-hand combat with the live-dead.

Slowly Mostyn and his people climbed the stairs, fighting off the reanimated dead every step of the way. Mostyn fired his pistol into the once pretty face of Patty Gibson, until her head was a shattered mess. Her snake-like body continued to undulate towards them until H'tha-dub dematerialized it away.

Jones fired the machine gun until it was empty. The pieces of what was once Eliza Pettigrew continued to hop, roll, and crawl after them.

H'tha-dub dematerialized the thing that was nothing more than two legs and two arms attached together and re-materialized it inside the stone wall. She did the same to the thing that was Evan Tanner's head and hands.

Using a sword Mostyn cut off the arms of what might have been Philip Grundseth, before H'tha-dub dematerialized it and rematerialized it inside the stone ceiling.

While H'tha-dub finished dematerializing the hacked up pieces, they sat on the steps catching their breath. A squad of OUP Special Forces arrived.

"About time you bastards showed up," Kemper spat out.

22

MOSTYN SAT in Doctor Bardon's office. The director of the Office of Unidentified Phenomena sat behind his large and heavy black walnut desk puffing gently on his pipe. For some time neither one said anything. The one who broke the silence, at last, was Bardon.

"No, Pierce, I am not going to accept your resignation." The director's tone was avuncular, almost fatherly. He went on, "For your information, I'm not accepting Doctor Kemper's either."

"She resigned?"

"Tried to. Just because you two had a misunderstanding is no reason why I should lose my best operative or scientist. We have important work to do here, Pierce. I don't have to tell you that, now, do I?"

"No, sir."

"Good. Enough of this nonsense. Come. Join me in a glass of port?"

Mostyn didn't care for port, but when it came to port no one said "no" to Bardon.

The director walked over to the sideboard that was now between the statues of Cthulhu and Shub-Niggurath.

"Lovely, aren't they?"

"Yes, sir." Although, if Mostyn were honest, he'd question why anyone would want such ghastly portrayals of evil around. Then, again, he wasn't Bardon, and the professor had a taste for such things.

The director poured out two glasses of port, sat in the dark chocolate leather chair next to Mostyn, and handed a glass to him.

The director took a sip. "She asks about you, you know."

"Who? H'tha-dub?"

Bardon grunted an affirmative. "You should see her. It would help her to acclimate."

"She'll see me?"

"Of course, my boy. She's in love with you. Ah, to be young again and have two beautiful women smitten by Cupid."

Somehow Mostyn couldn't imagine Bardon with a woman. He seemed married to his books.

Bardon sipped wine and continued his musing. "I suppose at some point you'll have to choose."

"Choose, sir?"

"My boy, have you heard anything I've said?"

"I thought so, sir. You mean make a choice between Dotty and H'tha-dub?"

"Yes."

"Dotty's done with me. She cleared her stuff out of my place."

"Oh, pshaw! My boy, she's just hurt. She's a normal, red-blooded American woman. Thinks she's all independent. Bah. She loves you. Just be patient. Before you know it, she'll be moving all her stuff back to where it was before in your place."

"How can you know that, sir?"

Bardon looked over the top of his glasses at Mostyn. "*You* are asking *me* that? You should know better, my boy."

The director sipped his wine, and Mostyn thought back to Dotty's comment about Bardon's voodoo being greater than God's omniscience.

Mostyn drank wine. "I hope you're right, sir."

"Don't worry, my boy. In the meantime, I think you should see H'tha-dub. Oh, incidentally, she's decided to take the name Helene Dubreuil."

"I see."

"We have paperwork being drawn up so she's an official person. Do see her."

"I will, sir." Mostyn finished his port in one gulp.

"The bodies of the two K'n-yanians were autopsied. Aside from larger brains, they're no different than you or I. I do regret we could not get more of the *y'm-bhi*. Fascinating. Simply fascinating." Bardon finished his glass of wine. "I hope Doctor Slezak is happy. She's a fine linguist. I'll miss her." Bardon got up and sat in his chair behind his desk.

"Sir, may I ask what you brought in to fight the K'n-yanians?"

"Wasn't enough. We installed some remote cameras to observe the field. You can imagine my surprise when they dematerialized that Class Six inter-dimensional drog-gaught. Thank God they're xenophobic. I don't think they'll be unsealing that tunnel."

"Probably not, sir. What about Obermaier and Bessemer Corporation?"

"They've closed up shop and moved their operation. Obermaier wasn't happy about it, but after he saw the video of what he was sitting on, he decided it was in everyone's best interests."

"A big bother, but certainly best."

"Now, my boy, you go see Helene Dubreuil and make up with her. She's going to be a tremendous asset. I'll have Agent Hollins take you to where we're keeping her for the time being."

He pressed a button on his desk and when Evelyn, his secretary, answered, told her to get Agent Hollins.

"You did a fine service for your country, Mostyn, in bringing us that wonderful young..." Bardon laughed. "Well, I guess she isn't exactly young at that, is she?"

"No, sir."

"Tremendous asset, then. Thank you for bringing her to us."

There was a knock at the door, and Agent Hollins appeared. Mostyn stood.

"Thank you, again." Bardon said.

"You're welcome, sir."

Mostyn, though, didn't feel good about any of it. He followed Hollins down the hall and out to a car. Betraying

Dotty and deceiving H'tha-dub... He sighed. He'd done it to get his people home. And they were home. In that, he'd accomplished his mission. He'd done his duty. Except for Slezak, but her choice was her choice.

As Mostyn was getting in the car, he murmured, "I hope she's happy."

"What's that, sir?" Hollins asked.

"Nothing, Hollins. Nothing at all."

EPILOGUE

HIGH ABOVE THE amphitheater a tiny drone sat anchored to the rock ceiling, its camera focused on the proceedings below. Miles above the chamber, on the surface of planet earth, and three states away, Doctor Rafe Bardon watched on the large screen the scene playing out far, far underground. With him was Helene Dubreuil. The camera zoomed in to focus on a woman tied to the table. The woman who was the attention of three men.

"That's B'ya-lub, the one who seduced Special Agent Jones in order to spy on him," Helene informed Bardon.

"She's speaking," Bardon said.

"Yes. We often do when under pressure or tremendous excitement."

"Are you able to read her lips?" he asked.

"Yes. She's begging them to have mercy. She's saying, 'I did as you asked.' "

They watched as the tongue was cut out of her mouth

and set aside. The camera shifted and focused on the table next to her. There, similarly secured, was Candy Slezak.

"She's not speaking English," Bardon said.

"No," Helene affirmed. "It's K'n-yanian. She's saying, 'Why are you doing this? I want to be like you! I'm not one of them! Please! Don't! Let me be one of you!' "

Filling the screen was the torturer's back, and then moments later he was holding Slezak's head by the hair. Her mouth still forming the words, "I'm not one of them!"

A WORD FROM CW

I hope you enjoyed *Stairway to Hell*.

If you did, please consider leaving a review on the site where you bought the book. It's free advertising for authors. And we appreciate it very much.

Become one of my VIP Horror Readers and you'll get the latest news from my world; plus curated content, free stories, and other good stuff.

Begin the adventure today and you'll get a copy of *The Feeder* (not available in stores) as my thank you.

Click, tap, or scan the QR code to become a VIP Reader today!

CONTINUE THE ADVENTURE!

Pierce Mostyn's paranormal investigations continue in *Terror in the Shadows*.

An eldritch terror. A lurking fear. And death on our doorsteps.

Special Agent in Charge Pierce Mostyn is on a collision course with a nightmare. And he doesn't know it. A gothic horror tale is being played out in the hills of Appalachia. Can he stop his team from becoming the next victims?

Click, tap, or scan the QR code to open your door to terrifying adventure.

BOOKS BY CW HAWES

CW is a multi-genre author.

The books below are portals to his many exciting worlds. And no AI was used in the writing of these books. Books by a human for a human.

Pierce Mostyn Paranormal Investigations

The X-Files meets Cthulhu. Pierce Mostyn does battle with inter-dimensional monsters bent on the destruction of humanity.

Nightmare in Agate Bay
Stairway to Hell
Terror in the Shadows
Van Dyne's Vampires
The Medusa Ritual
Demons in the Dunes
Van Dyne's Zuvembies

In the Shadow of the Mountains of Madness

Justinia Wright Private Investigator Mysteries

Justinia Wright is the PI with panache. These slow burn mysteries, written in homage to Rex Stout's Nero Wolfe, are sure to satisfy your craving for intriguing puzzles, quirky characters, and wise-cracking humor.

> *Vampire House and Other Early Cases of Justinia Wright, PI*
> *Festival of Death*
> *Trio in Death-Sharp Minor*
> *But Jesus Never Wept*
> *The Conspiracy Game*
> *A Nest of Spies*
> *When Friends Must Die*
> *Death Makes a House Call*
> *To Right a Wrong*
> *The Nine Deadly Dolls*
> *Ripples on the Pond*
> *Christmas with the Wrights*
> *Minneapolis's Finest*
> *Jack in the Box*
> *Sauerkraut Days*
> *Justinia Wright Private Investigator Omnibus Edition*

Magnolia Bluff Crime Chronicles

Tense slow burn mysteries set in our favorite town in the Texas Hill Country.

> *Death Wears a Crimson Hat*

Ten Million Ways to Die
Who Mourns Elektra?
Death by Moonlight

The Rocheport Saga

A post-apocalyptic adventure series in the style of cozy catastrophes such as *Earth Abides* and *Day of the Triffids*. Join Bill Arthur as he strives to build a new and better world on the ashes of the old.

The Morning Star
The Shining City
The Divided City
The Troubled City
By Leaps and Bounds
Freedom's Freehold
Take to the Sky

Decopunk

Alternative history adventures in a world where World War II never happened and swing is still king.

From the Files of Lady Dru Drummond
The Moscow Affair
The Golden Fleece Affair

Rand Hart Adventures
Rand Hart and the Pajama Putsch

Tales of the Macabre

For the horror lover in you.
> *Do One Thing For Me*
> *Metamorphosis*
> *What the Next Day Brings*
> *Ancient History*

Anthologies

Enjoy CW's stories in these short story collections.
> *The Phantom Games*
> *Beyond the Sea*
> *Overmorrow*
> *Arachnapocalypse! The Anthology*
> *Once Upon a WolfPack*

Available at your favorite online retailer. Just click, tap, or scan the QR code.

ABOUT CW HAWES

CW Hawes has written over 50 novels and shorter works of fiction. He was also an award-winning poet and had over 200 poems appear in ezines and and print.

He is a founding member of the Underground Authors and was the impetus for the highly successful Magnolia Bluff Crime Chronicles series.

After 35 years of working in county government, he retired at the beginning of 2015 and began a second career as a fictioneer. Perhaps some of the horrors Pierce Mostyn faces can be traced to his creator's own experiences in county government and beyond. Perhaps.

CW lives in Southern California. He enjoys reading, writing, chess and other board games, his daily morning walk, and contemplating the meaning of life while smoking his pipe. He also hasn't met a doughnut or a pizza he doesn't like, is something of a tea snob, and rocks out to Handel and Vaughan Williams.

You can get curated content and the occasional free story

when you join his mailing list, and you can reach him at his website, on X, and also Facebook.

To join his mailing list, click, tap, or scan the QR code:

To visit him on his website, click, tap, or scan the QR code:

To visit him on X, click, tap, or scan the QR code:

To visit him on Facebook, click, tap, or scan the QR code:

www.ingramcontent.com/pod-product-compliance
Lightning Source LLC
Chambersburg PA
CBHW061212170626

46809CB00003B/1328